Body Parts

By Larisa

ISBN 0-9760769-2-6
First Printing 2004
Cover art and design by Anne M. Clarkson

Published by:
Dare 2 Dream Publishing
A Division of Limitless Corporation
Lexington, South Carolina 29073
Find us on the World Wide Web
http://www.limitlessd2d.net

Printed in the United States of America and the UK by

Lightning Source, Inc.

~ Body Parts ~

Bloodshot blue eyes look down at the naked body of the victim; a hand covered in a surgical glove rolls the body from where it lay beneath the large oak tree in the dense woods along the Appalachian Trail. Revealed is a brutality that brings a grimace to the Detectives tired face. Her voice hoarse from too many hours on duty, she asks the first officer on the scene.

"Is the ME here yet?"

"Nope," The young officer cringed when silvery blue eyes shot through to his soul. "They're sending his assistant instead."

"You mean his flunky! God damn it, just what we fucking need, some damn weak in the stomach young punk." She stood up to her full six foot height and towered over the officer.

"No choice Detective Sallano, Doc had a heart attack last night, he's in the ICU."

She pulled the gloves off, stuck them into her pocket and then ran her long fingers through her below the shoulder length tangled dark hair. Sighing deeply, she tipped her head back trying to loosen the sore muscles in her neck and shoulders. "When the assistant gets here, I want to know the second the body is taken in and I want all the reports on my desk in the morning ya got that?"

"Yes ma'am, you want me to call you at home or have the dispatcher call you?"

"You call me at home, no matter what time it is."
She walked under the yellow crime tape and headed for the
dark blue Crown Victoria. Driving the fifteen miles to her
small house in the small town of Brunswick Maryland, she
pulled her car into the drive along side her house and got
out. Stretching her back and shoulders, a low groan escaped
when a sharp pain tore through her lower back and left hip.
Pressing on a pressure point in her hip, she fell against the
side of her car and swore. "Too damn old for twenty hour
shifts." Limping to the back door, she pushed it open and
her small furry dog attacked her. "OK, I'll feed you Bear."
She leaned down and scratched the cinnamon colored coat
of her Pomeranian. "I know I've been a rotten mother lately
but I'll make it up to you." She pulled a stick of beef jerky
from her pocket and handed it to Bear. Filling the large dish
with Bear's name on it with food, she filled the matching
water dish then headed for her bedroom, shedding her
wrinkled clothes as she went. Going out onto the small
deck that was off her bedroom, she turned on the Jacuzzi's
jets and sunk down into the water. A long deep sigh
bubbled from her lips as she sunk her head beneath the
water and stayed there for a few moments. This was the
only luxury she had in her home; she didn't see the need for
much in the way of extravagant things. She was a simple
person with simple needs; all she needed were the creature
comforts and her dog. An hour went by as she lay letting
the water jets soothe her aching muscles and frazzled
nerves. Climbing from the Jacuzzi, she wrapped a terry
clothe robe around her and headed to the kitchen for
something to eat and a much needed beer.

****

A bright desk light shinned down on to the cluttered
desk in the small 6x8 office in the back of the gloomy
morgue. The room seemed smaller because of the over

4

flowing boxes of files and personal items stacked against the walls, they all belonged to the retired medical examiner. Except for an over stuffed backpack with the name 'Brian' written across the flap in red magic marker that hung off the back of the old wooden desk chair. A sound came from the bay doors as they rose to admit the newest stiff as the medical examiners called them. The squeak of the gurney wheels echoed in the large room and then the sound of tennis shoes squeaking down the hall to the small office. A low groan came from the new Chief Medical Examiner as she dropped wearily into the hard chair. She had only been there one day and was already exhausted. In a period of twelve hours, she had performed four autopsies and signed numerous death certificates. She had applied for the position of assistant medical examiner the month before; she had been surprised when she received a phone call from the Hospital administrator the night before offering her the job as the new chief. She was saddened by the fact that she been hired for the position because of the former chief having a heart attack and retiring. However, she knew that some things happened for a reason. Now she would have to hire an assistant to help her because she couldn't do it all herself. That was something she was not looking forward to doing, all kinds of nut jobs wanted to work with the dead. Leaning back in the chair, she picked up the phone and called the number the young officer had given her. He had seemed almost scared when he handed her the number and insisted that she call it when the victim came in.

****

Detective Sallano rolled over on her worn lumpy couch and grabbed the phone off the end table, clearing her throat, she barked into the phone.
"Sallano!"
"Hello, this is the morgue. I was told to call you

when the Jane Doe was brought in."

"I'll be right there." She rolled onto the floor and crawled to her bedroom, she knew better than to fall asleep on the couch. With her bad back and left hip, she would be lucky if she would be able to walk afterwards. After dressing in faded Levi's, t-shirt and old work boots, she hobbled to the back door and out to her car. Glancing at the clock on the dashboard, she saw that it was close to two o'clock in the morning. "Jesus Christ what took them so long?" She muttered to herself.

*****

"What a rude person!" Brianna mumbled and hung up the phone; she went out into the large examination room and readied the body for the autopsy. Normally, she would wait until the next day to do the autopsy but with this being the third body in as many months with the same type of wounds. It was a priority case, or so the officer on the scene had informed her. Jumping up onto a nearby steel exanimation table, she lay down and closed her eyes; she intended to just rest her eyes until the Sallano person showed up. However, she fell asleep instantly.

****

Sallano pulled up to the dock for the morgue and looked around at the eerie place. Taking the steps to the door beside one of two bay doors, she went inside and followed the dark hallway to the autopsy room. Looking around, she saw two sheet covered bodies on tables. Going back down the hallway, she looked into the small office and found it empty. "Where the Hell is he?" She mumbled and went back down to the autopsy room to wait. Moving up to one of the tables, she leaned against it to take some of the weight off her left leg. Looking to the wall clock, she would give the ME ten minutes and then she would tear the Hospital apart looking for him. Forgetting what was on the gurney behind her; she put a hand back and felt the body beneath the sheet move. She jumped back and pulled her .357 from her shoulder holster. Taking a step forward, she grabbed an edge of the sheet and whipped it back from the body. "Son of a bitch!" Putting her .357 back in its holster, she shook the shoulder of whom she assumed to be the ME.

"Later baby...need sleep."

"I didn't drive all the way here so I can watch you sleep."

An eye peeked open and gazed with blurred vision at the tall dark women before her. "Uuhmm who are you?" A light blush covered Brian's face at being caught sleeping in the autopsy room. She asked as she swung her legs over the edge of the gurney.

"Detective Xepher Sallano, homicide, who are you?"

Brianna froze when she looked into the bluest eyes she had ever seen. "Sorry about that." She offered her hand. "I'm Chief ME Brianna Meadows." She jumped a little when the larger hand took hers. Covering the reaction by jumping off the gurney, she released Sallano's hand and walked over to the far wall for her apron and other items she would need. "Let's get started, I'd like to go home sometime in the next week." Xepher rolled her eyes at the attitude the young blonde headed medical examiner threw at her. As if she really cared if, she got to go home in the next week, month or year. She herself didn't know when the last time she was allowed to sleep more than two hours without someone calling her to report some kind of sick crime. Taking a spot on the other side of the examination table, she waited for Brianna to start.

Brianna couldn't believe how rude the woman was. *I didn't come all the way here to watch you sleep.* She repeated in a whiny voice in her head, she was exhausted and this was the last thing she needed. Watching the tall woman from across the room, she noticed the dark circles beneath her eyes and deep lines along side each corner of her pink lips. She also noticed how she favored her left leg by placing a good majority of her weight on the right side. Snapping on her gloves, she went to the table and drew the sheet from the body. Jumping up, she pulled down the microphone that hung from the ceiling and flipped the switch to the recorder on.

"Chief Medical Examiner Brianna Meadows of...Frederick County Hospital, the time is 0248, date June 26 2002, Case number 23672. Jane Doe. Deceased found in wooded area on the Appalachian Trail near the C&O canal. On initial exam, deceased is female between the ages of 21 and 30. Jane Doe was decapitated between the fourth and fifth cervical vertebra at post mortem. Tissue damage is ragged, showing that possibly, a serrated type large knife of saw was used." She looked up briefly through her face shield to see blue eyes studying her findings. "Tissues on remaining area show thoracic bruises and crushed trachea. Possible strangulation, will know further along in autopsy." Brianna moved down the body, using her hands, she palpated the ribcage, upper and lower arms to stop at the ends of bloody stumps where the feet used to be. "Broken second and third ribs on both sides of ribcage, along with bruising, hands and feet have been removed in the same manner as the head. Abrasions on elbows, knees and shines and what looks to be limestone dust ground into wounds?" Xepher was amazed that in just a short time the amount of information she was learning about the deceased. This was the first time that she had been in on such a detailed first examination. Most of the time, she listened to the ME say *"Ohh look they're dead. I'll send you my report in the morning."* Then she would have to track him down and practically hold him at gunpoint for details. Clearing her dry throat, she waited for the ME to look up at her.

"Was all the damage done post mortem and can you look at the back area and tell me why it was done?"

"The head was done post mortem but I can't really tell with the feet and hands yet. Most likely they were done while she was still alive." She took a deep breath and looked into tired blue eyes. "I looked at the back out in the field and what it looks like is that she was skinned of a tattoo." She rolled the body part way over and motioned for Xepher to join her. "If you look here at the edge over the right hip, you can see a small amount of black and red."

"So you're saying who ever did this wanted to make sure that we couldn't identify the body."

"Pretty much yeah, no finger prints, head, the works. I'll do X-Rays and see if they can be matched to any missing persons. Other than that," She shrugged her shoulders. "It's in your ball court Detective."

"How long has she been dead?"

"I'd say within three days or so. There's no lividity on the body anywhere. I'd say that she was hung by her feet when the head and hands were removed and then disposed of."

"How about sexual penetration, can you check and I'll be out of here." Brianna nodded her head; she went over to a table along the wall, picked up a small plastic evidence bag and a rape kit. When she was finished, she nodded her head and said that the woman had been penetrated both vaginally and rectally.

"I'll know more in the morning." She looked at the detective and saw the anger that filled her eyes.

"Thanks. When can I have the full report?"

"By noon tomorrow at the latest, you want me to send it to you?"

"No, I'll come by and get it." Without another word, she left the ME standing there.

****

9

Brianna placed the remains into the cooler drawer, shed her apron, scrubs in the biohazard containers and then went to the small office in a pair of boxers and t-shirt to start her report. She had no reason to go back to her small apartment; she had only lived there a little over a month since moving to Maryland from Ohio. She was living out of a suitcase and eating take out food when not looking for a job in the area Hospitals. The small single bedroom apartment still had boxes sitting all over the place for the simple fact that she didn't feel like unpacking. She didn't have enough room for all of her books and the clothes she did have could fit in a suitcase. Her main attire was surgical scrubs and lab coats. She had left Cleveland where she was an assistant medical examiner for Fairview Hospital because of a relationship with a doctor that became unhealthy. The older doctor became possessive and started stalking her during off duty hours. She had quit her job and moved out of the state after the woman attacked her one night outside of the Hospital and beat her to the point of Brianna ending up unconscious and rushed to surgery. Now weeks later, she was starting over and was not enjoying it at all. After turning on the ancient PC, she went to get a cup of coffee while it booted up.

*****

Xepher dropped face first into her bed still fully clothed, using her toes, she pushed her boots off and then rolled to her right side. Her hip was killing her and she knew that it was because of not getting any sleep. Reaching out to her alarm clock, she set the alarm to go off in two hours. That would give her 20 minutes to get to the office. If she was late, they could bite her ass. Dropping off to sleep, she dreamt of a little Medical Examiner with a nasty attitude.

* * * * * *

Brianna dropped into the wooden chair and started typing like a woman on speed. The thick black coffee was like drinking 10w100 motor oil and tasted just as bad, but it had given her enough of a caffeine boost to get the initial autopsy report started. She never bothered with listening to the recorded tape because she remembered everything about a case. That was one of the reasons she was able to skip two years of medical school and move up the ranks to become an assistant medical examiner before most others. One of her other talents was to be able to see things that others couldn't when looking at a victim. With the first two pages done, she saved it and then left the small office to go to a small room she had found earlier that day. It had a cot and a small table and chair in it. She wondered if maybe the former medical examiner used it to get rest during long workdays or when the weather was too bad to travel. Either way, she would use it when needed. Lying down on the small cot, her eyes fluttered close and she drifted off to sleep and to dreams of being in the darkness and excruciating pain.

* * * * * * * *

Xepher walked into her small cubicle and saw the folder sitting in the center of her desk. Setting Bear in her in box, she opened the folder and scanned the initial finds of the first officer on the scene. The body had been found by a couple of hikers walking the trail when they had stopped to rest, no evidence had been found at the scene as far as clothes or any other personal articles that would identify the victim. Pulling a dozen pictures from the folder, she spread them out on her desk and closely looked at each one. From what she could determine, the body had

11

been carried to the spot and laid the way it had landed on the ground when dumped. The Modus Operendi checked out to be the same as the other two bodies found in the area. Checking a map of the area, she noticed that a dirt road used for railroad maintenance was roughly a quarter of a mile from where the body was discovered. Pulling the other two files, she checked those off on the map as well. They were miles apart and showed nothing as far as a pattern except for the fact that they were all dumped around the C&O. Placing three pictures next to each other, she saw that two of them had areas of the body skinned. The last one the back from shoulders to hips and the other was the left calf area from back of the knee to ankle. As with the new body, hands, feet and heads were missing.

As of yet, none of the body parts had been recovered. They may never be and the bodies may remain as Jane Does.

****

A dark blue Crown Victoria cruised slowly along the streets of Hagerstown Maryland. The whip antennae bouncing with each pothole the tires dropped in to. The driver looked through the tinted windows at the prostitutes standing on the corners and up close to the doorways of apartment buildings and storefronts. Not seeing anything to his liking, he turned the next corner and got back onto the highway to leave the city limits. He knew that with the time of year, he would be able to find a young person walking the roads on their way towards the campgrounds in Frederick or farther west towards West Virginia. During spring break and summer, it was a time when the college students lived off the land and traveled by foot across the east coast. Taking a side road outside of Frederick that ran parallel to old Rt. 40 and to the Green Briar State Park. Taking a sharp right turn down through the large metal gates painted yellow, the driver scanned the areas with picnic tables and small two person tents. Flipping the blue lights on hidden behind the cars grill. He pulled over to where a young woman was pulling the stakes for her tent from the ground. Taking the nightstick from on the seat beside him, he slipped it into the plastic ring on his Sam Browne belt and left the car. Sticking his thumb on his left hand into the top of his belt and over his pistol grip, he had the other hand on his leather handcuff pouch. "Excuse me ma'am can I see some kind of identification?" The young woman looked at him quizzically, her dark brown eyes widened at the site of the tall officers hand resting close to his pistol.

"What have I done?" She asked while reaching for her wallet.

"Nothing ma'am, just checking for runaways, you resemble a young women that's missing. Could you take a seat in my car while I run this through the computer?" He took the license from her dirty hand and motioned to his car; he stepped beside her and opened the car door then closed it once she was inside. Getting back in the car, he glanced over at the nervous woman and reached for the radio microphone.

"Officer, I am not nor have I ever been a runaway. Besides, I'm 22 years old and not missing. Aren't you supposed to have a computer in here?"

"The department is a little behind in outfitting our cars." He keyed the microphone, reached for his nightstick and swung it at the young woman's head. A loud crack echoed in the car and the woman fell across the seat unconscious. The officer got out of the car, searched her campsite for her belongings and once he collected everything, he threw it all in the trunk of his car. Flipping the lights off, he left the park behind and drove off into the early morning hours.

*****

13

Brianna rolled from the cot and stretched her back and shoulders, shivering at the coldness of the room; she wrapped the thin blanket around her shoulders and left the room. Shuffling still half asleep to the Hospital cafeteria, she got in line for her breakfast. Loading her tray up with enough food to feed a small army, she carried it to a back table and sat down. She was halfway through her meal when the hair on the back of her neck stood up. Looking from beneath her lidded eyes, she saw a tall dark form at the coffee urn. Dropping further into her chair, she hid behind her coffee cup.

****

Xepher poured cream into the dark brew and watched, as the color didn't change one bit. "Shit will kill me for sure." She mumbled under her breath, handing a dollar to the cashier, she pocketed the four pennies she got back. "Price of crude oil's gone up again?" She asked and walked away with out getting an answer. Blowing over the edge of the cup, she let her pale blue eyes scan the room. They stopped when they found a tousled blonde head at a far table. Walking with a slight limp, Xepher stopped to stare down into guarded green eyes. "Dr. Meadows, can you answer a few questions for me?"

Brianna's voice was harsh when she replied, her eyes a dark angry green as they bore into Xepher's. "Don't you ever sleep or did you just stay up so that you could terrorize me on my second day of work."

"No, yes and yes." She took a seat across from the pissed off ME and set her cup in front of her. Pulling some papers from her pocket, she laid them out on the table. "These are the reports from the other two murders, what I don't understand is why there's no mention of the condition of the tissues around the amputated appendages?"

Brianna pulled the reports closer and scanned the information, her dark brows dipped down over the bridge of her nose. "Who did the autopsies?" She flipped through the pages again looking for the signature.

"I would take a guess and say that old creep that you replaced." She shrugged her shoulders and took a hesitant sip from the awful coffee. "I never got the full reports from who ever, I was told that they were confidential."

"That's bullshit," She looked up at Xepher. "How long have you been a cop?"

"Sixteen years why?"

"Then you should know that you get the full report not what the ME wants to give and there's nothing confidential about an autopsy report."

Xepher gave her a lopsided grin. "I know, and believe me I tried to get everything. And holding him at gunpoint didn't work because he called my boss and had me banned from the morgue."

"If you held me at gun point I'd have you banned to." Handing the papers back to her, she went back to eating.

"Are you always so rude?" Xepher questioned Brianna.

"Only with cops," Getting up from the table, she motioned for Xepher to follow. "Let's take a look at the files."

Xepher limped behind her mumbling under her breath about stuck-up doctors, and how she would love to plant a foot up a little blonde's ass. She jumped back a step when a small foot shot back at her.

"Same goes for tight ass cops, now be nice or I'll have you banned from my morgue."

****

They moved all the boxes of files into the small room with the cot so that they would have more room to search and to give Brianna more room in the tiny office. Brianna was at her nerves end, the filing system was like looking through a garbage heap. Nothing was in any kind of order and the files seemed dropped in any old box. She was finding files that were a month old in with stuff ten years old. With her hands covered in filth, she wiped at her runny nose and left it black.

"Detective this could take us days to sort through; Dr. Blane had no idea how to file anything." She tossed a stack of files into another box.

"I'm tempted to go to the ICU and shoot that son of a bitch!" She rubbed a hand across her face and left black streaks down her cheek and chin behind.

"Ohh please let me do it!" Brianna looked up and busted out laughing.

Xepher cocked an eyebrow over a bloodshot blue eye. "Has the stress gotten to you?"

"No, but you look like a zebra with those stripes on your face."

"I'd rather have stripes than a black nose."

"Goes with the job, I'm going to have to kiss ass to get some help in here and clean all this shit outta here." Getting up from the floor, she stretched and groaned. "I have an autopsy and a report to finish." She stopped at the door and looked back at Xepher. "Have fun." Xepher could hear her hysterical laughter all the way down the hall. Falling back on the floor in defeat, she lay there for a few moments thinking of what to do. A wicked grin came to her face, pulling her cell phone out; she called the station house and requested three uniforms to come to the morgue. With the help of three sets of hands, they would have the files sorted out at least by the year they were done.

****

Donning clean scrubs, her apron and safety shield, Brianna started on the Jane Doe from the night before. She examined the sites of the amputations closely and found that the head had been in fact removed perimortem and the cause of death. The hands and feet were postmortem. Shivers went down her spine at the thought of having her head cut off while she was still alive. It made her more determined to get a look at the other two cases to see if they were the same. If that were the case, this would be the first serial killer case for her. The only draw back that she saw was a certain maddening detective with beautiful blue eyes. An hour later, she had finished and was working on her report. The hair rose on the back of her neck and made her shiver. "I found them." Xepher said from behind her. Brianna tilted her head back to see a grinning detective waving two file folders in her hand.

"You found them in that mess? I'm impressed." She then saw the three uniforms walking behind Xepher and snorted. "You cheated!"

"Of course I did, I'm not stupid."

"Right." She went back to her report and ignored Xepher.

"Hey are you going to look at these or not?" Xepher stepped behind her and tapped her on top of her head with them.

"You know you're very pushy and irritating? And I'll look at them when I'm good and ready."

She dropped down close to Brianna's ear and growled. "No more than you are. I'm going to get lunch, I'll come back later for my report." She placed the files next to the PC and left. Brianna rubbed her grumbling stomach and sighed, she would kill for a meal not from the Hospital cafeteria.

"It's no wonder the former medical examiner had a heart attack." Brianna mumbled to herself. "That food up

17

there is something the EPA wouldn't touch."

*****

Xepher couldn't keep the grin off her face as she walked out into the parking lot. She was enjoying the butting of heads with the small medical examiner. She wasn't used to having someone go up against her at anytime, her stoic looks and intimidating ways kept most people at bay. Getting into her car, she drove to the nearest restaurant and went inside to order take-out. The cashier gave her the weirdest look when she ordered enough for four people. Taking the six bags of food out to her car, she pointed a finger at Bear. "You'll get yours when we get back to the Hospital." Her dog whimpered and begged so much that she gave in and gave her a piece of roll. "You have me whipped ya little shit."

****

Brianna pulled one of the drawers out containing one of the prior victims. With one glance at the ragged edges of the neck area, she knew that this victim was the same as the Jane Doe from the night before. What she couldn't figure out was why it was left out of the autopsy report. Looking down at the other report, she found the drawer number. Pulling it out, she grinned when she saw the same results. She now had three bodies with the same injuries. If not for Xepher questioning the reports, she may not have found them until too late if at all. The now recognizable feeling of Xepher being near had her turning her head, a raised brow over a green eye zeroed in on the bags in her large hands. "I have lunch and I'll even do something that I only do with my partner."

"What's that tease him with the food and not share so that he hates you as much as I do?" Brianna shot back.

18

"I'll have you know that my partner is a female and she likes me."

"She must be insane. Where is she locked in the car or up stairs in a straight jacket?"

Xepher brought a bag up to her chest and groaned. "Ohh you wound me with your razor tongue." She winked at Brianna. "She's out in the car waiting for the left overs." Green eyes caught fire, Brianna stomped towards Xepher and jabbed her in the chest with her index finger.

"You give your partner leftovers? I'm surprised she hasn't shot you yet!" She walked past her and down the hallway. "You know how hot is out there in a car? You dumbass cop!"

"She can't come in here!" Xepher yelled and went chasing after her; she stopped inside the door and groaned when she saw Brianna looking through the window of her cruiser.

"There's no one in there!" She turned and glared at Xepher. "And why is your car running you lying sack of shit." She planted her hands on her hips and glared.

"Because the air conditioning needs to be on that's why."

"So that the delicate flower that you are not doesn't have to get into an oven of a car?"

Xepher raised an eyebrow at the insult. "You are so good at insulting me, is that the reason you're a doctor for dead people because you have a rotten bedside manner?"

"I'll have you know that I'm a nice person, I just don't like you!" She rattled the locked door handle and jumped back when she heard a deep growl come from inside. "What the Hell is wrong with your partner?"

"Nothing, she hates blondes." Brianna snorted at her, walked over to Xepher and stuck her hand into her front pocket to search for her car keys. "Hey! What the Hell are you doing?" Xepher felt her face turn red with arousal from fingers fumbling in her pocket.

"Getting your keys." Pulling them out, she waved them in front of Xepher and went back to her car.

Xepher's eyes closed and her head fell back. "Ohh man, don't open the door." The second the car door opened a furry cinnamon tornado jumped out, raced to where Xepher was standing and jumped at the bags of food in her hands. "Now you did it." She raised the bags above her head.

"Your partner is a dog?" Brianna busted up laughing; she couldn't believe that the stoic detective had such a small dog.

"Yeah, gotta problem with that? Since you let her out, you can share your lunch with her."

****

Xepher felt betrayed, her precious little dog was sitting on Brianna's lap and was quietly waiting for pieces of the baby back ribs that she had brought from the Outback restaurant. No matter how hard she tried, she just couldn't be mad at either one of them. "So did you finish my report?"

"Yeah and I'll have you know that all three bodies are here. I found the other two in storage and the wounds are the same." She filled her mouth with food and waited for Xepher to say something. When she looked up, she saw the normally pale blue eyes were silvery. A fear rose inside her at the sudden change in the tall detective.

"Son of a bitch! Why was that left out of the report?"

"Don't know, maybe Doc Blane didn't think it was significant." She knew something was wrong with leaving the information out of the report but had no idea of why he had done it.

"Is he out of the ICU yet? I wanna know why he did it!"

20

"Not as far as I know. Remember, I've only worked here two days."

Xepher felt her phone vibrate against her hip, answering it she barked out her name. She listened for a few moments, grunted and hung up. "We may have a name for one of the earlier bodies; a fax just came in from Pennsylvania about a missing Grad student that never returned home after she hiked out here last month, the X-Rays are being sent courier service to you." She put her trash in a bag and stood up from where she had been sitting on the floor. "I have to head back to the office, let me know if you get anything."

"As soon as I get them, I'll check. Thanks for lunch."

"No problem." Xepher walked from the small room and heard the clicking of toenails on the floor behind her. "Come on Bear, we have lots of work to do, you little traitor." Brianna stood in the hallway smiling as she listened to the tall detective talk to her dog. The woman was defiantly strange and not as stoic as she wanted people to believe. Her little dog was proof of that. Not as if Brianna cared either way, her history with cops made her leery and untrusting of their work ethics. She returned to the small office and pulled up the latest autopsy files from the last month. Typing in the case number she hit enter and waited for the PC to kick out the results. When the file came up, she compared it to the copy that Xepher had found. She double checked it twice and noticed that the reports were completely different. On the first victim, it stated that the cause of death was asphyxiation due to bursting capillaries in the eyes. She knew that was wrong since it didn't have a head. The second report read that extensive bruising around the larynx and throat was conclusive with strangulation. "How the Hell can you say that when there's no damn neck!" She had a bad feeling that she had just walked into a very bad nightmare. Checking her in and out boxes for any paper work that needed completed, she signed a few lab reports and then went back into the autopsy room and pulled all three bodies from the storage drawers. Lining them up side by side, she pulled a clipboard from a drawer and started taking notes as if she were doing the first preliminary report.

****

Dropping behind her desk into her worn office chair, Xepher booted up her PC and waited. She looked at Bear who was spinning in circles in her in box before she dropped down with a low snort. "Rotten little traitor, made me look bad in front of Doc." Her words hit her and she wondered why it mattered what the doctor thought of her. The woman could skin her with a razor tongue quicker than anyone she knew could and with a glance; she had her heartbeat slapping her ribcage. She dropped her forehead on to her desk when the memory of a small hand scrounging around in her front pocket had her center thumping with her heartbeat. "Gods I don't need this, not now after all these years."

"Need what, your head examined?"

Xepher raised her head enough to see a pale yellow dress shirt and the tip of a pale blue tie. "Captain, I can't believe your wife let you leave the house dressed like that." She rose up and leaned back in her chair.

"Like what?" The older gray haired man looked down at himself. "I don't see anything, my flies closed, shoes match and I think my jockeys are on right."

"Ohh never mind, just loose the tie before you clashing kills one of us." Picking up a rawhide chew, she spun in through her fingers waiting for her Captain to give her the bad news as he always did. "Soooo?"

"Sew buttons on your underwear." He remarked and

dropped into the chair next to her desk. "Get anywhere on the new case, I called you at home and then found out that you were at the morgue bright and early."

"We may have identification for one of the victims; I'll know as soon as Brianna...I mean Doctor Meadows takes a look at the X-Rays."

"Doctor Meadows, where's Blane at?" She filled him in on all that had happened over the last two days and how she had come across the complete files on the other two cases at the morgue. She asked him if any one else had complained besides her about reports being sloppy, inaccurate or incomplete. "Ohh just a few guys, but it was nothing that harmed any of their cases. Why?"

"Nothing matches between the bodies and the reports and I want to know why." Her voice had deepened and her expression became dark and dangerous. "How many more victims were there that I don't know about?"

"Check with the other detectives and see if they have anything not solved that matches what you've got." She nodded her head and grumbled about never taking a vacation again until she retired. She had been forced into taking a two-month vacation due to an injury while apprehending a man who had killed his wife and mother in-law. No matter how much she fought, the doctors refused to release her back to full duty. Even a desk job was out of the question for her and them. So now, she was trying to catch up with everything that had happened while she was gone.

✳✳✳✳✳✳✳✳✳✳✳✳

The dark blue Crown Victoria pulled around to the back of the two-story house in Burketsville Maryland. The officer got out and went into the house by way of the back door that led into the large country kitchen. Taking the servants stairs to his bedroom, he quickly changed into a dark green uniform with a patch over the left breast pocket

23

that said Jeff's lawn maintenance. Running a comb through his thin brown hair, he splashed after-shave on and went back downstairs to find his mother. At the age of 40, he still lived at home because his mother was in her 70's and had health problems. It used to bother him that he was trapped living at home but since she became wheelchair bound, he found that he had more freedom to live as he wanted. During the hours, that he worked a nurse came into check on her and made sure that she took her heart medicine. Once home, he took over until she retired for the night. Making his way through the dark house, he heard the low murmur of the TV set and followed it to the small setting room that she stayed in during the day. He remembered having to stay in the same room when he was growing up, never allowed to run through the house as other children did or go out and play under the clear skies. For hours after school, he would sit in the small chair against the wall and listen to her preaching about the sins of man and how her son would never be like his father. She would describe his father as a sinful man that only wanted to experience the flesh of women and take their pureness. Many nights, he would sit naked in the chair while she showed him pornographic pictures of men and women coupling. If he got an erection, she would hit him with a ruler across his penis until the erection went away. He remembered pissing blood and being so sore that he would cry at night in his small bedroom upstairs. After months of conditioning, he no longer had erections period. He would have thought that his mother would be proud of him; instead, she felt that he was ready for the next step. One day, she had him bend over the chair and lay upon his stomach. Using a long piece of rope, she bound his hands and feet to the chair. He knew better than to ask her why. He screamed out in pain when she forced the plastic end of an enema bag in his rectum. For hours, she forced it in and out of his body until he had passed out from the pain and blood loss. Now as he looked at the frail birdlike body strapped into the wheelchair, the rage boiled inside to the point that he wanted to do to her what she had done to him. He was now the caregiver and the preacher of sin. What stopped him was that she was no longer aware of what went on around her. A series of strokes left her to nothing but a shell of a human. He often sat and stared at her empty eyes and wondered if it would be better to suffocate while she sat in her chair. "Hello mother how was your day, I have a new girlfriend." He sat down across from her and looked for some kind of emotion from his words. "She will be cleansed like all the others, I will drain the sin from her body and show her the way of living in purity." He cackled at the drool slipping down the old woman's chin. How he hated her for all she had done to him, it made him ecstatic to see her so helpless. He left his mother sitting in the dark room and headed out to his car. Opening the trunk, he pulled the bound and gagged young woman out and carried her down to the cellar. Flipping the bright florescent lights on in the center of the room, he lay her down onto the stainless steel autopsy table. Then went to prepare for his night of ritualistic fun, striping down to bare skin, he danced around the room to religious music coming from the small CD player in a corner of the room. Pulling a leather strap from under the table, he fastened it around the waist of the frightened woman. "Don't be afraid, when I'm finished you will be a pure as the driven snow. All those sinful thoughts about sex will be erased from your mind." Using a filleting knife, he cut the duct tape that bound her feet and then used the leather straps attached to the end of the table to hold her legs splayed apart. After he had her hands fastened, he used a pair of surgical scissors to cut her clothes off and threw them into the old coal furnace against a far wall. Standing at the end of the table, he examined her athletic build and made a harsh noise through his nostrils. "Disgusting whore!" He screamed at her so loud that she flinched and closed her eyes. Pulling a drawer out from under the edge of the table, he waved a disposable razor in front of her eyes. "To be pure is to be pre-puberty." Forcing her legs further apart, he roughly shaved her pubic area not caring if he cut her. Cries muffled from behind the duct tape across her mouth, tears flowed down her cheeks and into her hair as she tried to move away from him. "I'm not hurting you! YET! With pain comes pureness!"

****

Brianna finished with doing the autopsies on the other two bodies over again. She knew that she could be fired for doing it but at this point the injustice of what Dr. Blane did, weighed more on her mind than anything. Because of his incompetence, if that in fact is what it was? The police would have known everything from the beginning and they may have already apprehended the murderer or been able to investigate into the purchase of weapons with serrated edges. Now they would know what to look for as far as type of weapon used and other consistencies overlooked or ignored from before. She would need to get in contact with the maddening Detective and relay the new evidence that she had found. Going into her small office, she searched for the piece of paper that had Xepher's phone number on it. After searching the entire place, she came up empty handed. "You dumb shit call the police station, but which one?" She pulled a phone book from a desk drawer and saw all the phone number listings for all the different agencies in the area. "Pick one and maybe they know who she is and can give me her number. It's not like she's one you would forget, tall, gorgeous, striking blue eyes...I'm talking to myself and getting hot over that damn woman!" Calling the first number on the list for the Frederick police department, she spoke to an officer at the front desk. He knew who Sallano was but didn't know if she was in the building. The best he could do for her was to call the homicide division and leave a message. "That's fine, if she can't reach me here at the morgue, this is my home phone number. Tell her to call no matter what time it is." She repeated her home number twice to make sure that he had it right then hung up the phone. She sat few a moments in the peace and quiet for a before she called up to the ICU ward to see how Dr. Blane was doing. The runaround she received from the head nurse had her temper flaring. She locked her office door and took the steps up to the ICU ward. Following the blue line on the wall, she spotted the nurses station and a nurse whom she thought she had just spoken with. Stomping up to the nurse, she made it a blatant point to look at her nametag. "Nurse Reynolds, I'm Dr. Meadows, I just called up here to check on my colleague. I would appreciate the fact that I am a member of this staff and am entitled to have my questions answered to the best of the staff member's ability. Now where is Dr. Blane's room and his chart?" The young nurse was at a loss for words, no one had ever read her the riot act before.

"Excuse me Dr. Meadows, but I don't know who you are or what kind of doctor you are?"

"What the Hell difference does it make?" Brianna threw her hands in the air. "I'm the Chief Medical Examiner, so that means I out rank most of the bags of hot wind here. Never mind I'll find his room myself." She pushed past the nurse and wandered down the hall looking at the names on the charts outside the doors. She stopped at the last one and was spun around by a young intern.

"I'm sorry but you can't go in there. He's very frail and needs his rest."

"What is it with you people here? Have I dropped into a *Robyn Cook* medical mystery or something? Since when can't another doctor look at a patient?"

"Ma'am, you're the coroner."

"Yeah and I know just how to kill you so that no one will ever find any evidence or your body! Now get the fuck out of my way!" She pushed him away from her, took Blane's chart and walked quietly into the room. She heard voices out in the hallway and then the squeaking of shoes on the tiled floor. Scanning Blane's charts, she looked at the blood tests and noticed that there were elevations in some of the lab results that couldn't be explained. She took the folder down the hall to the nurse's station and ran copies of the chart off. Sticking them in her pocket, she replaced the chart next to Dr. Blane's door and was met halfway down the hall by a Hospital security guard.

"Ma'am I need you to come with me please."

"What the Hell is it with this place? Am I being arrested?"

"Just come with me ma'am."

Her green eyes blazed, her breath ragged from the rage she was feeling from her roughshod treatment by all her so-called co-workers. "Fine, let's go!" The security guard tried to take her by her arm and found, that she maybe a small woman but she could knock him on his ass. She jerked her arm hard enough from him that he stumbled. "I want to see the Hospital administrator!" She growled.

"Sorry ma'am but he's not in right now." He took her all the way to the emergency room and escorted her out the doors. She spun on her heel and faced him with her arms crossed over her chest.

"What the Hell is this, are you kicking me out?"

"Yes ma'am, I was told by the chief resident to escort you from the Hospital."

"Under what reasons, I work here you stupid ass!"

"Sorry ma'am you'll have to come back on Monday and speak with the Hospital administrator. There's no record of you working here."

Brianna threw her hands in the air and howled. "Fucking asshole men!" She stomped off towards the parking lot where her car was and then remembered that her keys and everything were in her office. All she had was the key to her office and her useless ID badge. "This is a fucking nightmare!"

****

"Hey Sallano, you have a pissed off woman on line three!" Xepher looked up from her paperwork to one of the other detectives.

"She say who she is?"

"I am not asking her anything! That woman's insane; I'm deaf in my ear now1"

"Ohh for Christ sakes, you men are useless!" She snagged the phone and barked into it. "Sallano!"

"You had better come and get me, because I'm on my last damn nerve and I'm going to commit premeditated murder! DO YOU HEAR ME!?"

Xepher yanked the phone from her ear and looked at it with raised brows. The voice on the other end was still screaming at her.

"I'm going to zap every single one of my co-workers with 2 million joules and watch them turn into crispy critters!"

"Brian will you calm down," Xepher whispered over the phone. "Give me ten minutes and I'll be there. Don't kill any body; I have enough paperwork as it is." She heard traffic in the background and became confused. "Are you still at the Hospital?"

"No, I'm at a pay phone in front of the Dollar store."

"Just hold on and stay out of the street." She picked up Bear and ran from her office. She had no idea what was going on with the medical examiner but if she was threatening mass murder, then something was wrong. She started to laugh when she pictured the small doctor chasing

29

nurses through the hallway with the paddles in her small hands. "Shit, I'm as bad as she is!" She got into her car, hit the lights and sirens and tore down the street towards the Hospital. Rounding a corner, she saw a couple of punks running towards her trying to flag her down. She ignored them and continued on her way with the punks running behind her car. "Is there supposed to be a full moon tonight or something?" She saw a fight up ahead on the sidewalk in front of the store Brianna was supposed to be. "Ohh shit!" She stopped her car up on the sidewalk and slide across the hood to pull Brianna off a teenager. "Brian!" She struggled with the small woman who was punching the shit out of the kid. "BRIAN!" She yelled into her ear as she wrapped her arms around her, lifted her off the ground, and stumbled to her car. Opening the passenger door, she forced Brianna in and closed the door before going back to where the kid was laying on the ground gasping and holding his broken nose. "What's going on here?"

"That crazy bitch jumped me!"

She turned her head when she heard the whirl of the window going down. "Don't you get out of the car!" She pointed a finger at Brianna.

"That little fucker was robbing the store! Arrest him!"

"You were robbing the store," She cuffed him on the side of his head. "What's wrong with you?" She pulled her handcuffs from their pouch and cuffed him to the guideline for the telephone pole. "You know she's suffering from PMS and if I hadn't come along, you would have been the fourth guy she killed this week." She left the teenager lying on the ground with his mouth hanging open.

She turned in her seat to look at the red-faced medical examiner. "You're in the wrong line of work." Her eyes grew wide with the thought of Brianna having a gun. "Changed my mind, you with a gun is too scary to think about."

"Ohh fuck you, now get me out of her before I go back out there and beat someone else up!"

"Let me call this in first." They waited for a uniformed officer to pull up behind them, Xepher told him what happened and for him to take the punk in and bust him for the collar. She pulled her car back onto the street and headed for a small coffee house that she stopped in every morning on her way to work. She glanced over at Brianna and snorted. She met fiery green eyes and winked.

"Don't start with me!" Brianna growled. "I'm tired, hungry, pissed at the world and want to beat someone up!" The car stopped at the side of the building, Xepher turned in her seat to capture green eyes with her pale blue.

"I was right about your bedside manner wasn't I?" She wasn't prepared for Brianna to launch herself across the car and pounce on her. She felt a sharp pain above her right breast and yelled loud enough to send Bear scurrying into the back seat. They wrestled on the front seat until the driver's side door opened and a uniformed officer peered in at them.

"You need some help Sallano?"

She looked up from where she had Brianna pinned to the seat. "Nah just had to force her to take her prescription." She looked into dark green eyes. "Prozac wasn't it?" Her answer was snapping teeth and a deep growl. "Thanks, we'll be alright as soon as it kicks in."

Brianna snarled and bared her teeth. "You just wait Xe! When you least expect it!"

"Next time you bite me Brian, make it lower." She got off her and then pulled her from the car. "Come on I'll buy you a coffee and donut."

"Figures you'd bribe me with a donut after police brutality."

"You're the one who bit me. I was just restraining you."

"More like humping me."

Xepher snorted and raised a dark eyebrow at her. "Believe me; I prefer a bed over the front or back seat of a police cruiser. And who says that I would want to hump you?" She gave Brianna a huge smile that dimmed the sun and left the small woman speechless. Brianna kept glancing sideways at her on their short walk to the coffee house. She couldn't get her heart to stop pounding erratically, their wrestling match had her aching in places long forgotten.

She called me Xe; no ones ever called me Xe before. Xepher's mind was spinning with thoughts of lying across the spitfire medical examiner. She would have no problem doing anything with the little doc anywhere and she knew it. A heat flooded her senses as she held the small hand in hers, she didn't remember when she had taken her hand but wasn't about to let go even as they went into the coffee house. She led them to a table in the back and sat with her back to the wall. She had a phobia of not being able to see who came through the door and gave Brianna a funny look when she squeezed into the booth beside her.

She narrowed her eyes at her. "I like my back to the wall, so get over it."

"No problem." She ordered for them and sat quietly thinking of everything that had happened in the last couple of days. Taking a deep breath, she picked up the scent of a light musk perfume and Aussie shampoo. Stretching out her long legs, she groaned at the sharp pain in her hip.

"You dying?"

"If I said yes, you'd be happy. So no, I'm not."

"Damn, just my luck, I'm stuck with super cop and her Pomeranian sidekick."

"I got the short end of the deal here, you're nuts and you attack innocent police officers."

Green eyes filled with flames, Brianna jabbed her in the ribs until she yelped. "Are you calling me short?"

"See you just admitted that I'm innocent." The grin never had a chance to form on her face; Brianna wrapped an arm around her neck and put her in a headlock. Xepher gave her no fight what so ever when she found her face pressed against soft breasts. The waitress shook her head, placed a plate of pastries and their coffees on the table.

"Hey Xepher no breast milk with you double mocha."

Brianna let Xepher get up from where she had been holding her down. "You want to explain that remark?"

"Nope." She picked up her coffee, took a small sip, and ignored Brianna.

"Nope, what kind of answer is…?" She replayed the sentence over in her head. "Breast…milk…grrrrr." She looked to a grinning Xepher who wiggled her dark brows. "You could have told me!"

"Ohh yeah, like I'm gonna say to a strange person. Ohh by the way I'm a dyke and I like breast milk with my mocha."

"I see your point…you just called me strange didn't you? Never mind."

Xepher hid her grin behind her coffee cup and fought not to have coffee shot out her nose when Brianna gave her a dirty look. "What happened today that you wanted to kill everybody?"

"Today, I think it started yesterday when I met you?" She took a deep calming breath and released it through clenched teeth. "I found all kinds of stuff wrong with the reports, autopsies, files and you can name just about anything and it'd be wrong to." She told Xepher everything she had found while examining the other two bodies and comparing the reports she had found to the computer reports. Then about trying to see Dr. Blane in the ICU and finished with her being thrown out of the Hospital until Monday when she could straighten every thing out with the Hospital administrator.

"We can always sneak you back in through the door off the dock."

"Nope, I locked it when I was done."

Xepher rubbed her jaw with long fingers while she tried to think of how to get Brianna back into the hospital. "OK how about the other doors; they can't be watching all of them."

"If it's like the other hospital I worked in, they lock the front door after a certain time and the only way in is through the ER. So, I'm screwed until then."

"I can get in; I'll just go and get your stuff."

Brianna shook her head and sighed. "I don't know if you've noticed but the doors all have those security locks on them. You have to use a badge to open them and…"

"Yours doesn't work because you don't work there according to them."

"Exactly, I've been using my keys to get in the back door until they could fix it in the computer, which the administrator was supposed to have done today!"

Xepher leaned her head back against the booth, tilted her head to the side to look at Brianna's profile. "Getting out of a state pen would be easier than getting into the morgue."

"I could always sit on the dock and wait for a meat wagon to pull up."

"Nah, come on lets get out of here." Dropping a twenty on the table, she waited until after Brianna got out of the booth, took Brianna's hand and led her from the coffee shop. "You can stay at my house tonight and we'll figure out something tomorrow."

****

They rounded the corner and pulled up Xepher's driveway, Brianna looked at the small house and then to the detective. "I figured you for a big huge butch log cabin."

"Nope, I like the simple things." She parked the car, got out, and waited for Bear and Brianna to join her at the back door. "I only have one bedroom, the other is my

34

office." She pushed the door open and waited for Brianna to walk through. "You can have my bed and I'll sleep on the couch."

"I can't take your bed." She argued and lost when she realized that Xepher was not going to give in. She got the nickel tour, a t-shirt and shorts to sleep in.

"Go ahead and take a shower if you want, I'll be out on the deck if you need anything." Xepher limped towards the sliding glass doors leaving Brianna to her own devises. Turning on the Jacuzzi, she shed her clothes and let them drop in a heap on the deck. Slipping into the water, she closed her eyes and let the warm water and pulsing jets relax her aching hip and lower back.

*****

Brianna took in the large modern bathroom and thought of her small apartment. Adjusting the water, she undressed and stepped into the shower and let the water beat the exhaustion from her tensed muscles. When she felt the water growing cold, she stepped from the shower, dried off and dressed. She listened for Xepher but heard only silence. Going out the door she had seen Xepher use, she stopped dead in her tracks. The tall detective's eyes were closed and a soft snore came from her parted lips. Brianna moved closer, letting her eyes trail over the sharp features of high cheekbones and strong jaw. She felt a pull deep in her chest to let her fingers caress the woman's face. Her breath caught when the clouds moved from the full moon and cast a silvery glow across her. Her heart jumped when Xepher's eyes opened and took on a glow that shot straight to her soul. Stuttering over her words, she spoke in a soft tone. "I ahhh…was just going to…wake you." She looked everywhere but at Xepher. "You may drown in there."

"That would be bad." She tried to get up but slipped back down into the water with a deep moan. Resting her

35

head on the edge of the Jacuzzi, she waited for the pain to go away.

"Are you alright?" Worried, Brianna stepped closer and placed a hand on Xepher's muscular shoulder. "What's wrong?"

"Just old," She rose up from the water and sat on the edge. "It gets worse when the weather changes." She swung her legs over and eased up to her feet. Limping into her bedroom, she leaned against the wall until the pain subsided. Brianna stopped beside her and looked down to see a scar that went from her pubic bone up over her left hip to end at her lower back. Tracing a finger across the pink scar, she watched as goose flesh rose across the skin.

"What happened?" She asked and helped Xepher over to her bed so that she could sit down.

"Got shot bringing in a murderer." Unashamed of her naked body, she closed her eyes, fell back onto her bed with a low groan, and lay with her arms over her head.

Brianna sat on the edge of the bed next to her, took in the full extent of the scar, and saw the dips in her hip where the muscles had been damaged "Where was your partner when you were doing this?"

"He was the one I was trying to bring in; he killed his wife and mother in-law and then called me and told me what he had done."

Brianna felt tears building up in her eyes; she couldn't imagine the emotional or the physical pain of what the detective dealt with every day. The only person cops truly trusted were their partners and then to have that person shoot you. "I'm sorry." Was all she could say, she wiped the tears from her face but not before blue eyes saw her.

"It's OK, it happens sometimes." She pushed herself up and grimaced from the sharp pain. "Got a new hip joint out of it, just wished the damn thing didn't hurt like a bitch."

"Hold on a minute, lie on your stomach and let me try something." She held up her hands when blue eyes narrowed at her. "I'm a doctor remember, I'm not getting fresh with you, I promise." She helped her roll over. Slapping her hands together to warm them, she laid them on Xepher's lower back near the scar. Using a slight pressure, she pressed with the heels of her hands until she felt the muscles relax under her fingers. Moving them over the long muscle of her glut, she pressed with her fingers in a pressure point and felt Xepher's body go rigid.

"That hurts like a bitch."

"I know it'll go away in a minute." When she felt her body relax, she pressed on another pressure point and waited. She finished her treatment with a massage of the affected area. Don't move just yet, she massaged her leg all the way to her ankle and pressed pressure points at the area near her ankle, outside and inside of her foot. When a low sigh came from the detective, she smiled. "Feel better?"

"Yeah it does." She rolled over and eased up from the bed with very little pain. Taking her robe from the foot of the bed, she pulled it on and sat back down. "Where'd you learn pressure points, I know you don't need them on dead people." Brianna's face paled at the question, her hands started to tremble and tears flowed down her cheeks. Xepher was at a loss. "You don't have to tell me, I'm sorry if I hurt you in any way by asking."

"It's OK, it's still painful." She looked into confused eyes. "Let me show you, it'll make more sense." She stood up, turned her back to her and lifted her shirt to show a long scar running the length of her back along her spine. Pulling the left side of her shorts down, she revealed a scar that ran from her hipbone to mid thigh. She felt warm fingers touch the scared area and looked to see pale blue eyes taking in the spots where metal pins had been sticking through her flesh.

"What happened?" She raised her eyes to misty

37

green.

"Hit by a car in the parking lot at the Hospital." Rearranging her clothes, she sat down next to Xepher. "That snapped my leg; I had a compound break in the femur and some damage to the tendons and ligaments around the hip joint and knee."

"But the scars up your back, what did they do there?"

"That was from the baseball bat that was used to try and kill me after I was hit by the car." She took a deep breath and willed the emotional pain away; she had not spoken to anyone about what happened that night except for the police who did nothing about it. Xepher took her hand and held it between hers; they both had a lot of emotional and physical scaring that made them who they were. Hers was from trying to prevent her partner from taking his own life and Brian's was from someone trying to take hers. "One of the reasons I left Ohio and came here was I had been having a relationship with a doctor. Everything was going fine at first, dinners, movies, and staying up late and just talking. Everything changed the fist night we became intimate." She felt the blush work its way up her neck to color her face. With bashful eyes, she glanced quickly to see Xepher paying close attention. "While I was at work the next day, I kept getting phone calls every ten or fifteen minutes. Who ever it was kept hanging up on me; finally, I stopped answering the phone. If it was something important, the Hospital would page me." She moved back on the bed so that she had her back against the headboard. She continued with her story after Xepher stretched out beside her and lay with her head resting on her palm. "When I got home the phone was ringing, the biggest mistake of my life was answering it. My new lover ripped into me for not answering the phone at work and wanted to know who I was fucking behind her back." She cast a sideways glance to see if Xepher had caught on to what she had said. A faint flicker washed through blue eyes at the mention of her lover being female. "I calmed her down and told her that I would talk to her the next afternoon. Everything was fine for about two weeks and then it started all over again, phone calls, dropping by the morgue to make sure I wasn't doing anything wrong, following me when I left the Hospital, sitting outside my house all night and threats against my life."

"Did the police know about all this?"

Brianna gave out a short bark of a laugh. "I called them, went to the station, filed complaints, told them about stalking laws and even had a restraining order put against her! You know what they said?

"They couldn't do anything until she hurt you bodily."

"You got it! It took her running me over with her car and using a baseball bat to damage my back bad enough that now I have a steel rod in me."

"This woman, where is she now?"

"Living her life as if nothing ever happened," Wiping the tears that flowed down her face, she tried to stifle the sob that wanted to come out. She had never cried after what happened that night. Her rage at the injustice done to her would not let her. The gates flew open the second she felt arms wrap around her and pull her against a warm body. It felt like forever that she cried into Xepher's chest. Wiping her eyes and sniffling, she pulled back and looked down at her hands. "I'm sorry, I don't even know you and I'm crying all over you."

"It's OK, sometimes that's the only thing to do is sit and cry."

"You don't exactly strike me as the crying type." She said softly.

"I'm not; I go out and arrest bad guys instead."

"Maybe if you'd been around I wouldn't have had to go through what I did." She rolled to her side and looked up into Xepher's compassion filled eyes. "They didn't even arrest her because no one saw her do it; it was my word against hers."

"I don't understand, even after all you did with the restraining order and complaints."

"She's the head shrinker for the police department, they seemed to have lost all the reports and she had a solid alibi for that night."

Anger filled Xepher's eyes, turning them to a silvery color that sent chills up Brianna's spine. "Fucking assholes!" She growled. "What about getting a lawyer and fighting it, you had your copies right?"

"Xe, that crazy bitch's father is a judge."

"Now I know why you hate cops, I want you to know that I do what ever I can to keep people safe. Right now I would do anything to catch that psychopath out there killing women." She fell back on the bed and grumbled under her breath. "I just need one little thing to steer me towards him." Brianna got off the bed and went to where she had left her scrubs, she returned with a handful of papers. Sorting through them, she handed a majority of them to Xepher.

"Those are the preliminaries that I did on all three of the bodies and full autopsy reports." She gently gripped Xepher's hand. "Xe, he cut their heads off while they were still alive."

"Holy shit!" Her eyes were wide and a disgusted look came onto her face. "What kind of sick fuck am I looking for?"

"A very dangerous one, I need to get into my office or into my apartment. I have on CD every known weapon or instrument, I can match the wounds to a weapon and maybe you'll be able to track that down."

A dark brow rose over a narrowed eye. "You're not a normal medical examiner are you?"

"No and you're not a normal cop, you have your

good points."

The tall detective grabbed her chest and gasped. "A compliment! I don't believe that came from your mouth, I'll have you know that I have many good points."

"And an ego the size of the moon," She got up from the bed and went to the bedroom door. "Good night Xe, I'm stealing your dog." Whistling for Bear, Brianna dropped down onto the couch, pulled the little dog to her chest and breathed in the scent of Xepher's cologne that lingered on her dog. "Your momma is something." She spoke into the soft fur and drifted off to sleep.

****

Xepher lay across her bed thinking of what just happened. "She stole my dog." A grin came across her face then faded as she looked at the reports in her hands. "You have your good points too Brian." For hours, she combed over the reports and made notes of things to check. This was the first time she had ever seen such a detailed autopsy come from the Frederic Hospital. When her eyes started burning, she gave up, flipped the light off and drifted off to sleep with the facts of the murder case's running through her mind.

****

The phone rang waking Xepher from a troubled sleep, blindly reaching for the annoying receiver, she barked into it.

"Sallano!"

"Sallano, this is Jenkins. We've got a murder over at the Hospital."

Xepher rolled over onto her side and looked at the clock. "Why are you calling me, can't someone else get it?"

41

"I think you want to see this one...it's the medical examiner."

Her heart slammed in her chest, dropping the phone on the bed. She jumped from her bed and ran to her living room, she breathed out a sigh of relief when she saw that Brianna was asleep. Going back into her bedroom, she picked up the phone. "The medical examiner is here with me, so she's not dead."

"It's Dr. Blane; someone decapitated him in his Hospital room."

Rubbing her forehead, she groaned. "OK, give me a half hour to get there. Don't let anyone in there, close it off and put a guard on the door."

"I have to warn you that some nurse at the Hospital said she saw a blonde haired woman leaving the room."

"When? Before or after he was murdered?"

"Afterwards."

"Shit! I'm on my way."

Hanging the phone up, she quickly dressed and went to wake Brianna. Leaning over the sleeping woman, she shook her shoulder. "Brian wake up."

Brianna mumbled into Bears fur. "No more sex, need sleep."

"Sex? Can I share your dream?" Her dark brows rose over amused eyes, she shook her harder and tried again. "This is a sex free zone, wakey wakey, dead bodies to look at!" Leaning close to her ear she yelled her name and jumped back to avoid having her face busted when Brianna leapt from the couch.

"I hate that!" She rubbed her eyes with her fists. "You just lost points."

"Someone killed Dr. Blane, he's missing his head. Let's go."

"But I'm not dressed!" She ran after Xepher.

"Can change on the way." She was out the back door before Brianna could utter a word. Running to the

42

bathroom, Brianna grabbed up her clothes and shoes and ran through the house and out the back door to the waiting car. She shot a glare at Xepher, pulled the t-shirt over her head and tossed it into the back seat.

"Do you ever get to sleep more than a few hours?"

"Nope, I would if people would stop killing each other." Flooring her car, she whipped around the slower moving vehicles and took the exit to the Hospital. Sliding to a stop outside of the ER doors, she was out and jogging to the doors with Brianna still trying to get her shoes on. She yelled at the tall detective and swore that she heard a growl come from her.

"Xe damn it wait up!" She caught up to her with her shoestrings trailing behind her. "If I fall and break my neck, it's your fault! And you drive like a maniac." Flashing her badge at the guard near the front door, they took the stairs to the floor where the ICU was and saw a cluster of people standing in the hallway. Xepher reached down, took Brianna's hand in hers and led her through the throng of people. Nodding to the officer standing guard, they went to the door and stopped at the threshold. The walls splattered with blood, the sheets and floor soaked in it.

"What a fucking mess." Xepher mumbled under her breath. "We need some gloves and booties."

"I'll get them, be right back." Brianna left her side and went down to a supply closet for what they needed. Xepher leaned as far as she could into the room to get a better look at the blood patterns on the walls. From in the hallway, she heard yelling and knew it could only be one person that could yell that loud. Leaving the room, she saw that a uniformed officer had Brianna up against the wall and was cuffing her.

"What the Hell are you doing?" She asked the officer.

"A nurse just identified this woman as the one she saw leaving the room of the deceased."

43

"Bullshit!" Brianna yelled and struggled against the cuffs.

"Yeah it is." Xepher pulled her towards her and took the cuffs off. "When was this that Dr. Meadows was supposedly here killing Dr. Blane?" The officer pulled out his notebook and checked his notes.

"About 50 minutes ago, she said, she was wearing a white lab coat when she saw her."

"Tell that nurse to get her eyes checked Dr. Meadows has been with me since 5 O'clock this evening." She rubbed the reddened area around Brianna's wrists. "I want the security tapes from this floor for the last 24 hours." She wrapped an arm around a pissed off medical examiners shoulders. "I want all these people out of here except the ones needed to run the floor. Come on Brian; let's get the supplies we need." They waited while the police photographer took pictures of the room, when he was finished. Brianna called the time of death and filled out the necessary paperwork that both she and Xepher would need. They then checked for trace evidence on the victim, bagged his hands, wrapped the sheets and blankets around his body. Diagrammed the blood splatters, and took sketches of the room before they moved the body to the morgue. While they had been in the room, the Hospital administrator was called. He was standing in the hallway waiting for Xepher when they pushed the gurney into the hallway. Her stance showed the coiled power her body contained, eyes silvery with rage, she pinned him where he stood with a glare. "You had better inform your people that Dr. Meadows works here and get all the shit straightened out in the computer! You have screwed up my investigation because some asshole threw her out of the Hospital! Now fix it or I'll arrest you for impeding a murder case!" She pointed a finger at the officer who had tried to arrest Brianna. "I want that door sealed and guarded. NO ONE and I mean it, goes into that room but me or Dr. Meadows."

44

****

A huge grin split Brianna's face when they stepped into the elevator. She reached up with one arm, pulled Xepher down to her and kissed her cheek. "You just moved up on my hate list."

Xepher ran her fingers across the tingling flesh of her cheek and her eyes twinkled with surprise. "What happens when I reach the number one spot?"

"Ohhh I give it a thought or two about maybe liking you." When the door opened, she pushed the gurney down the dim hallway to the autopsy room. "I'll take a look at the wounds and do the autopsy tomorrow. I'm in no shape to work this early in the morning." She spent 30 minutes examining the body of Dr. Blane, when she was done; she pushed the body into a storage drawer and went to find Xepher. "He used the same weapon on Blane as the others." She looked around the small office they were in for her backpack. "Did you see my backpack?"

"Nope, wasn't in here when I came in. Did you put it in that little room?" They searched the small room and didn't find Brianna's backpack, they went back to her office and checked every corner and came up empty. Brianna checked the top drawer of her desk where she had put her keys and swore. "My keys are gone." She slammed her palm down on her desk. "My backpack, the keys to my car and apartment."

A panicky feeling tore through Xepher, her instincts were telling her that this was not a coincidence. "Are there security cameras down here?"

"No, there's really no need for them." She moved closer to Xepher, fear showing in her eyes. "Do you think who ever killed Dr. Blane took my stuff?"

Xepher wrapped an arm around her and led her from the morgue by way of the back door. "I think so." She

45

scanned the area around the dock and small parking lot. "What kind of car do you have?"

"A burgundy Prelude, I parked it over..." She looked around the parking lot and didn't see her car. "They stole my fucking car!" She was on the verge of throwing a world-class temper tantrum when Xepher pulled her into her body.

"Hold on Brian, let me call and see if it was towed away." A few minutes later, Xepher told her that her car was in the impound lot at the police station. A Hospital security guard had it towed because there was no parking sticker in the window. "We'll go get your car later right now I'm ready to drop from exhaustion, let's go home." She realized what she had said and smiled, it sounded so right for her to say that to Brianna. "I'm warning you now, Bear's sleeping with me."

"We'll see about that Xe."

****

Dressed in tattered clothes, Dundee hat and old combat boots, "The Preacher" as he liked to call himself ran the brush through the fur on the red fox he had just finished mounting on a piece of drift wood. From a young age, he showed an interest in taxidermy. Finding animals on the road became hard, so he then started killing neighbor's pets and stuffing them. One day he was strangling a large dog. And became so excited sexually by its struggles that he gave up on looking for road kill or poisoning in favor of using his bare hands. By his late teens, he was torturing prostitutes and leaving them dead in the motel rooms for other men to take the blame. With the last one, he had killed by strangling her with a thick gold chain that was around her neck. Her skin tore beneath the chain and coated the preacher's hands with blood. His release ripped through him when the coppery scent reached

46

his nostrils. With her last breath, the prostitute prayed for his soul before her eyes turned vacant. It was then that he knew what he must do; purge the world of sin by spilling blood. Taking the red fox on its wood to a mid high shelf, he sat it next to the severed head of Dr. Blane. He didn't want to kill the man but he knew too much and was getting too nosy where his sisters, the preacher's mothers health was concerned. He had hoped that his little experiment with certain herbs in the old man's coffee would have killed him instead of just giving him a heart attack. Now his problem was even larger, he picked up the backpack with the name 'Brian' written across the flap. At first, he thought it to be a man until he found the wallet inside and saw the young woman's picture on her driver's license. He would have time enough to take care of her when he disposed of the last woman he had brought home.

****

It was past eleven o'clock when Xepher woke to Bear whining close to her ear. Pulling her pillow over her head, she whined back at her. "Go wake Brian up, she can let you out." A smile came to her lips when she thought of the small feisty blond sleeping on her couch. No woman had ever stayed at her house before; she found that she wished it were permanent. When Bear pounced on her head and bit at her fingers, she rolled from beneath the sheet and staggered through the house. She stopped to look over the back of the couch at Brian and grinned. During the night, her shirt had crawled up her body to show her Sylvester and Tweedy bird underwear. Snickering, she went to the kitchen and unlatched the doggy door for Bear. Starting the coffee pot, she pulled a bag of bagels from the refrigerator and laid them on the table. Fifteen minutes later, she had bacon and eggs cooking and had just poured a cup of coffee when a still asleep Brian came into the kitchen snarling.

47

"Do you have to sing so damn loud?" She bared her teeth at Xepher before she sat down. Xepher turned to lean against the counter, a brow raised above an amused pale blue eye.

"I've never known anyone who hates everything."

"Don't hate everything, just you."

"I thought I was moving up the list?"

"You are but I still hate you." She sniffed the air and grinned. "You can cook?"

"Of course I can cook, doesn't mean that I'm gonna feed you."

"Feed me or call 911."

"Why 911?"

"Because me and kitchens don't get along, three alarm fires are nothing compared to what I can do with a toaster."

Xepher placed two bacon, egg and cheese bagels on a plate in front of Brian and then added a cup of coffee. "You know you're fun to tease." She stood by the French doors to the backyard, the light coming in shone through the white button down shirt she had slept in. The sight of her firm breasts pushing against the thin material had Brian choking. Xepher moved quickly to her and smacked her between her shoulder blades. Handing her a glass of water, she leaned down to look into tear-filled eyes. "You OK?" Brian looked down the front of the opened shirt and started choking again; water came out of her nose and mouth. Xepher tipped Brian's face up and used the tail of her shirt to wipe her face. "You're not allowed to die at the kitchen table, so what's all the choking about?" She followed misty green eyes downward to the area between her thighs. "What, did I miss something when I shaved?" She ran her fingers through the strip of dark hair and snorted when Brian began to cough and turn a deep red. Tousling Brian's messy hair, she left the kitchen. "It's almost noon, I'm going to shower and dress. Brianna had no idea what had gotten

48

into her, she had seen Xepher in all her naked glory the night before and had no reaction as she just did. Wiping the sweat from her upper lip, she shivered from the heat between her thighs.

"I'm beginning to really hate her...a lot!" She jumped when Bear came charging through the doggy door and started to give out piercing barks at the door. Going to the door, she pushed the curtain back and looked out to see an older man with a paper bag in his hands. She tapped on the glass and mouthed the words "Can I help you?" He held a badge up to the window and yelled he needed to see Sallano. Opening the door, she let him in and gave him a curious look.

"I'm Captain Boggs, Sallano's boss."

"Ohh OK, I'm a homeless person." She grinned up at the older man. "I'll go get Xe for you."

Boggs shook his head and took a seat at the table. "Homeless person...Xe? Ohh is she in trouble." He chuckled.

****

"Hey Xe! Your Captain's in the kitchen!" She peeked around the corner of Xe's bedroom door and watched transfixed as Xe pulled a pair of skintight faded Levi's on.

"Boggs is here?" Xepher turned and started to walk past, but a pair of small hands on her hips stopped her.

"Button your shirt." Green eyes bore into her. "You're not going out there until you button your shirt." She huffed and did it for her.

"You had better go put some clothes on...suuufffriiing succotash." To get her point across, she lifted the bottom of Brian's shirt and pointed to her underwear. "May give the old buzzard a heart attack."

"I'm first in line." She mumbled to herself and then

49

searched through Xe's drawers for a pair of shorts to wear. When she returned to the kitchen, Xe gave her a raised eyebrow. The Captain noticed as well and couldn't miss the chance to tease Xepher.

"So XE, you're dressing the homeless women now?"

Dark brows gathered over her straight nose, then the left one rose when she saw the mischievous grin on Brian's face. "She's gonna be more than homeless when you leave." She gave Brian a lecherous look. "Boggs, this is Dr. Brianna Meadows the new medical examiner, dog thief, tease and she hates me." She turned to her smiling boss. "What brings you to the house of terror?"

"I have a shit load of files, the security tapes from the Hospital and X-Rays that the courier couldn't deliver. Because you probably had the ME tied to your bed."

"Not yet I haven't but the day is still young. Let's go in my office and take a look at what you have there." She grabbed Brian's ass as she went past and ended up with a foot in hers. "Ya hate me?" She asked over her shoulder.

"More than ever! Where's MY dog?"

****

Boggs and Xe sat in front of the small color TV in her office and looked at the security tapes. They came to one part and froze the frame. "That's the last person to see Dr. Blane alive." Boggs said. "From the report I got this morning, some nurse identified Dr. Meadows as the killer."

"It wasn't her; she was with me at the time of the murder. Plus look at the person here…Brian come here a minute." They waited for her to show up in the doorway and Xe told her to stand there a second. "Now look where the suspects head is on the doorframe and look where Brian's is." Boggs compared the differences. "There's a good two foot difference in their heights."

He nodded his head. "And this is not a woman, the back and shoulders are wide like yours." He gave her a wicked grin. "You're built like a guy I can't help it."

"Not from what I've seen she's not." Brian ducked from the room and went down the hallway howling.

"So you were the one tied to the bed, must be loosing your touch XE."

"Was not nor ever have been. Now she's got you calling me Xe, in three days she's turned my world upside down."

"Seems to agree with you though." He ignored her low growl. "Now, these files I have, I just picked up this morning. I had them forwarded from other precincts." He flipped the one on top open and pointed to the date. "I called the chief there and he said that you can come up and take a look at what ever they have."

"I'll go today after I drop…shit I can't leave her alone." She pinched the bridge of her nose and explained to Boggs about Brian's backpack and keys being stolen from her office the night of Dr. Blane's murder.

"I'll put a uniform with her when she's at the Hospital and then have the uniform take her home afterwards." Brian wasn't to happy about the arrangement that the Captain had set up, the only cop she trusted was Xepher but there was nothing she could do about it. She couldn't take the chance and lose her job because of a psycho stealing her keys and she was afraid of being in her office alone. Therefore, she would just have to deal with it the best she could. She had lots of work to keep her mind off the problem and knew that would help.

****

The drive to the Morgantown police station took six hours; Xepher could hardly get out of her car when she got

51

there. Her hip and lower back were killing her; she leaned against her car for a few minutes until she could deal with the pain. She wished that Brian were with her to hit the pressure points and take away the pain. The thought of Brian being alone with just a uniform cop, bothered Xepher more than she liked to admit. She felt that she should be protecting her and no one else. Hours later, she had gone over every file they had, including the autopsy reports. There were similar things with the case but she didn't have the feeling in her gut that she relied on. She would take the files to Brian and let her look over the autopsy reports and see what she thought of them. She was beginning to rely on the doctor for her knowledge among other things.

      Brian compared the X-rays from the Captain with the X-rays of the three women; she double-checked them again and sighed when she found that there was a match. She knew it meant closure for the girl's family but it also meant that they had lost a loved one for good. She would let Xe know when she got home that night. Home was not her apartment, which she couldn't get into anyway. Calling the apartment maintenance man, she explained to him what happened and arranged for him to change the locks on her door, to install a dead bolt and to leave the new key in an envelope in her mailbox. She was not about to take a chance on the psycho having a key to her apartment. Next was seeing if the uniformed officer with her could get someone into make a new key for her car that was still at the impound lot. After batting her lashes at him, she thought that he would fall over trying to get to his cruiser to call the police mechanic. When he came back in out of breath, he told her that her car would be delivered to the Hospital with new keys. *"Ya still have it Brian; you can make them swoon with your charm."* She thought to herself then mumbled under her breath. "Too bad it doesn't work

52

on someone else." Going back to her paperwork, she signed off on papers for the lab to run tests on blood samples of Dr. Blane. When she had performed his autopsy, she examined his heart and found no disease or reason for his heart attack. There was very little plaque in the arteries and the muscle was that of a younger man. She still thought that the previous test results showed something strange. She took more samples and sent them off to be checked for natural and organic materials. It was a gut feeling that made her do it and she never second-guessed that. Placing the closed file on the identified body, she scrawled across the top half of the folder the girl's name. Picking up the phone, she called the girls next of kin and waited for the phone to be answered. She usually let the police call the parents but she needed to know something for her report. "Hello this is the Chief Medical Examiner Dr. Meadows. Is this Mr. Levine?"

"Yes, is this about my daughter Laura?"

"Yes sir it is, I'm sorry to inform you of this over the phone, but I have identified remains here in Frederick Maryland as belonging to your daughter." She waited a few minutes and then proceeded with her questions. "A question if I may; can you tell me where she was during the time of her disappearance?"

"She was with a group of college students walking the Appalachian Trail. She had called us two days before she disappeared and said that they were camping along the river and that she would be heading home by the end of the week."

"Did she say who she was with dorm mates or acquaintances did she have a boyfriend? And how exactly was she going to get home?"

"She was with some kids she knew from campus. She didn't have a steady boyfriend and that she was going to catch a ride, I presumed that she was going to hitch hike the same way as she had gotten down there."

53

Brian was shocked, she hadn't even thought of the victims hitch hiking. "Thank you sir, I will pass all this information onto the investigating officer." She finished the call by taking down the information for transporting the remains and expressing again how sorry she was for their loss. Replacing the receiver, she leaned back in her chair and let ideas run through her head. "Wonder if I can track down who she was with? I need to know if she had a boyfriend or significant other with her." She was startled when the uniformed officer stepped into her office and handed her keys to her car.

"The shop just dropped it off, the mechanic said that everything is fine with it and the new keys work."

"Thanks, I appreciate what you did very much." She shoved her new keys in her pocket and gave him a smile as he left her office.

****

A loud roar echoed in the cellar, the preacher fell forward from where he straddled the woman's limp body. His body jerked and trembled with his release. The pruning saw clattered to the floor, he smeared the warm blood over his chest and genitals and felt his scrotum clench tightly. Gripping his testicles in a blood covered hand; he squeezed until another release burst from him and his semen spurted out to fall on her unmoving chest. Collapsing onto her cooling body, the preacher rested until he was able to catch his breath. Rolling to his feet, he pulled a hose down from the ceiling, turned the sprayer on and watched as the blood ran from the dead woman and washed down the drain in the autopsy table. When she was completely clean, he stood in the center of the floor over a steel grate and washed the blood from his own body. Looking to the pale body, he felt his penis throb and come back to life. Slapping it as hard as he could with his hand, he flinched and gasped at the pain.

Reaching for the disposable razor he had left near the table, he started to shave his pubic area of all stubble. He ignored the nicks to his skin as his blood mixed with hers and went down the drain. When he was finished, he pulled her by her arm until she fell to the floor. Dragging her to a makeshift altar, he positioned her so that her body was resting on forearms and knees. He screamed at the top of his lungs to the rough hand drawn picture on the white washed wall. "I have made an offering of this sinner to you; she is now cleansed of all sin by the letting of blood!"

****

Brian thanked the officer as he walked her up to her door; she had a feeling that the young officer was smitten with her and turned down his offer to come inside. After she convinced him that she would be all right, he went back to his cruiser and waited until she was inside before leaving. Flipping the light on, she went to her answering machine and saw that no one had called her. Not surprising since at this time, she had no one besides Xepher in her life. Dropping the files she had brought home on top of a nearby cardboard box, she went into the kitchen to see if she had anything to fix for supper. It was well past six o'clock and she had yet to eat anything since that morning. Finding nothing of interest, she headed to her bathroom for a long bath and maybe take-out later. She immediately thought of Xepher and wondered if she would join her for a pizza and beer. Flipping the light on, she gasped and stepped back into the hallway. With the eye of a medical examiner, she could tell that no one had been killed in her bathroom, but had washed the blood of another off. The sink, floor and bathtub had smears of blood. Lying on the floor in a bloody heap were surgical scrubs, booties and a white lab coat. "That son of a bitch is trying to frame me!" Going into the kitchen, she picked up the phone and dialed Xepher's cell phone number. She was thankful that she had asked for it earlier that day in case of an emergency. She waited for it to ring and prayed that Xepher was either on her way home or already there. She didn't want to call the police station and have all kinds of cops traipsing through her small dumpy apartment.

"Come on Xe answer the damn..."

"Damn what Brian?'

"Thank the Gods! Get over here now, that fucker was here and left my bathroom full of bloody smears."

"Where's your apartment?" She asked as she slowed down in case she would have to cut across the grassy median strip. Once she had her address, she took off in the direction she had been headed. Brian only lived ten minutes at the most away from her. Turning down a side street, she shot across and pulled up in front of the small apartment building next to a burgundy Prelude she assumed was Brian's. She wondered how she had gotten her car back and was a little afraid to ask her. But right now, what weighed heavily on her mind was that Brian's apartment had been broken into. She ran up to the door, pounded once before the door was ripped open and Brian pulled her through.

"That son of a bitch was here last night! What if I had been here when he showed up!?"

Xe saw Brian's walls starting to crumble. Pulling her into her arms, she rested her head on top of hers and just held her.

"Did you go in the bathroom?" She heard the low mumble of 'no' come from where Brian had her face pressed against her breasts. "Let me call this in and get the photographer over here and the tech guys." She pulled back just enough to look into frightened green eyes. "I don't want you staying here. I want you at home with me, OK?" With the nod of Brian's head, Xe placed a soft kiss to her forehead and pulled her back into her body. Pulling her cell phone from her belt, she called the station and then took Brian into the kitchen. Opening up the cabinet, she pulled down two coffee cups and readied the coffee maker. The whole time she kept glancing at the still woman sitting in a chair quietly. Moving behind her, she wrapped her arms around her and pulled her back into her body. Leaning down close to her ear, she whispered. "I won't let anything happen to you, I give you my word." Burying her face against her neck, she stayed that way until she heard the doorbell ring. Kissing Brian's temple, she left her to answer the door.

****

"I want pictures of everything. I want fingerprinting, fibers, and vacuuming of the floors in the bathroom, hallway and her bedroom." When she had everyone doing what she wanted, she returned to the kitchen to check on Brian. Her mind was reeling with how close she had come to maybe losing the small doctor. She knew in her heart and mind that she was lost to the argumentive, stubborn headed, sharp-tongued little blond. She would do everything in her power to keep her safe.

****

Brian sat with her face buried in her hands, she was trying to hold herself together but it was getting harder by the second. She felt invaded both emotionally and personally. In all the years she had been a medical examiner, no one had ever done what this murderer had. She had no clue as to why he had come into her apartment and tried to frame her. She was on the verge of tears when, she felt Xe come up behind her to enfold her in her strong arms. Xe pressed her body against Brian to share her warmth. The one thing she now knew was that, she could count on the detective's strength and friendship. Both times that she had needed Xe, she had been there in record time and offered comfort and understanding. "Let me get us some coffee and when the guys are done we'll go home." Brian loved the sound of the word home; a small smile came to her lips. She glanced to her left and watched her stoic friend prepare their cups. She couldn't believe that Xe knew how she liked her coffee made. Not even her own mother knew that she like both cream and sugar. Turning back to where she could see the techs working, she wasn't paying attention when Xe jumped back and slammed the refrigerator door. "Son of a bitch!" She growled. "Don't open that." She pointed to the refrigerator and left the kitchen to get a tech in there. Brian could only guess as to what was in there. She knew if she had opened and found something gross, her cussing would be heard clear to the West Coast. Sighing, she took her cup of coffee and sipped the brew without cream. "Bag it and everything else in there, I don't want to take a chance on having him screw around with her food. Take everything to the lab and tell them to test for every known biological and natural substance not normal for the article."

"Got it detective, I'll stay there until it's all written up." He opened the refrigerator and swore under his breath. On the top shelf were a pair of hands placed together as if they were praying. He carefully placed a bag over them and lifted out the chilled flesh.

"Guess he knows about my cooking skills huh?" Brian was doing her best not to freak out and run screaming from her apartment. She knew that she would never be able to stay here now she would look for a new place to live as soon as she had a chance. Tomorrow was too late as far as she was concerned.

"Are you guys done in her bedroom?"

"All done, just be careful of the fingerprint dust and

the luminal. We found some blood where it dripped from his hands or what ever."

Xe took Brian's hand and led her to her bedroom. "Get some clothes and what ever else you might need, and then we'll go home." Brian took a total of fifteen minutes to collect all that she needed, including her laptop and the CD's she needed. With everything stuffed in a gym bag and her laptop case slung over Xe's shoulder, they left the apartment with Xe giving orders to the techs to lock it up when they were done.

****

"Do we have to go home right away?" Brian asked as she moved closer to Xe inside the cruiser.

"No, where did you want to go?"

"A bar, preferably a gay bar." She looked at Xe's strong profile and saw a small smirk form on her face.

"Are you going to get drunk and take advantage of me?"

Snorting out a laugh, Brian busted her bubble. "You wish I could get that drunk."

"And all this time I was under the impression that I was irresistible."

"You're dog doesn't count and she likes me better anyway." *You are way beyond irresistible! You're the most beautiful woman I've ever seen.* She said to herself and felt a deep blush work its way up her neck. "I need a strong drink and to relieve some stress."

"Relieve stress, how do you relieve stress?" Xe's heart stopped and was on the verge of shattering into tiny little pieces. *Please don't tell me it's by picking up some slag and screwing her in the bathroom!*

"Dance my fool head off, that's how."

****

Xe pulled her cruiser into the parking lot, turned the engine off and then turned to look at Brian. She could see the stress in her features, deep creases along the sides of her mouth making her look like she was scowling. "This is the only place I know of, it's not fancy or anything but they do have good music."

Dark green eyes moved from where they were looking out the windshield to connect with silvery blue. A small smile came to Brian's face almost erasing the tension and stress. "Good, cuz I'm going to dance until I either drop or someone throws me off the dance floor."

"Are you saying that you suck when it comes to dancing?"

"You'll just have to watch and rate my abilities for yourself." She didn't give Xe a chance to say another word nor get around the car to open the door for her.

****

Xe stood at the end of the bar drinking a Jack Daniels neat and watching Brian clear the dance floor. She was having problems with her heart beating against her ribcage to the point of pain. She could feel moisture building between her thighs and soaking her Levi's from watching Brian gyrate on the dance floor. The sensual way Brian's hips swayed to the music made her mouth go dry. Taking a sip of her drink, she watched Brian turn away a woman who approached her. She did the same two more times before one of them came up to her. "Can I dance with your wife?"

With surprise shinning in her pale blue eyes, she asked. "Dance with my wife?"

"Yeah, the hot little blonde, she said I had to ask you first."

60

"She did? Sorry but this dance is mine," She placed her glass on the bar. "Maybe I'll let you dance with her later." She left the woman with an envious look on her face. Making her way to the dance floor, she stopped and watched Brian for a few minutes before she stepped up behind her. Placing her hands on her hips, she pulled her back into her body. Leaning down close to her ear, she purred in a deep sensual voice. "Will your wife be pissed at me for dancing with you?"

Brian brought her hand up and placed it at the back of Xe's head, pulling her closer she purred back. "That depends on how we dance." She turned in Xe's arms, ran her hand up her chest to linger on her cheek before brushing her bangs back from her darkened blue eyes. "Are you any good?"

"Ohh I'm bad...very bad." She moved closer to Brian, running her hands up her back and back down to cup her firm ass. Slipping one thigh between hers, she stepped forward and pressed against her.

"Forget my wife; I'm going home with you." She wrapped her arms around Xe's neck and pulled her closer. A low moan came from her when Xe moved her hands up to caress her back and started to sing to her as they slow danced.

Love sure is something no one can explain
It can bring you such joy, it can bring you pain
And with every emotion, love puts us through
There's nothing you can say, when love finds you
Love is the power that makes your heart beat.
It can make you move mountains,
Make you drop to your knees.
When it finally hits you, you won't know what to do,
There's nothin' you can do when love finds you.

Brian felt tears forming in her eyes as she listened

to the words of *Vince Gills* song, she pressed her face deeply against Xe's neck and ran her fingers through her silky hair. The only word that came to mind was "Destiny." The last chorus went straight to her heart.

And when you least expect it, it will finally come true
There's nothing you can say when love finds you

When the song ended, Brian pulled back and looked into dark blue eyes. What she saw there was pure unconditional love. "I hate you Xe." She leaned up and brought their lips together for a lingering kiss. When they came apart, she whispered in a low voice. "I really hate you." The kiss she gave Xe had the tall detectives knees going weak, their tongues seeking out each other and caressing. Moans rumbled in their chests as embers burst to flames and scorched their senses. They never noticed when the music stopped or the lights came on signaling that it was closing time.

"Out! Come on everyone clear out!" The bouncer yelled at everyone standing around. Xe felt a tap on her shoulder, breaking the kiss, she growled at the interruption. "Move it."

"I'll move it all right," She gave the bouncer a glare. "Home to our bed." Wrapping her arm around Brian's waist, she walked them to the door. Just as she stepped outside, her cell phone rang. "Son of a bitch!" She flipped the phone open and yelled into it. "What now I'm busy!"

"Not yet you're not." Boggs said. "We have another body; it's near Cindy D's restaurant up behind the liquor store in the trees."

"Son of a bitch! When I catch this guy I'm gonna rip his head off and ram it up his ass!" She felt Brian fall against her side and whimper. "We'll be there in 45 minutes." She was ready to go on a rampage, her body was humming from arousal and there was not a damn thing she could do about it. Taking Brian in her arms, she buried her face against her neck and moaned. "Gods I'm so sorry. We have another body."

"When you catch him, I'm going to help you kill him! I'm dying here!"

"Makes two of us," She stepped back and took her hand. "Let's get this over with so we can go home."

****

Blue lights flashed and bounced of the liquor stores wall, the low murmur of the police radios droned in the background. Xe and Brian could see uniformed officers keeping the gawkers at bay, while the Chief spoke with a handful of reporters. Stopping the cruiser close to the other squad cars, they got out to see the yellow crime tape strung across a large area in the back. Xe went to the back of her car and opened the trunk for the stuff they would need. She treated each scene that she went to as if she was walking into a sterile area. With Hospital booties, surgical gloves and her hair pulled back in a ponytail. She wanted to preserve the evidence as best she could and leaving her own trace evidence only made it harder on the techs. Taking a black nylon bag from the trunk, she handed it to Brian.

"What's this?" Brian asked as she held up the heavy bag.

"Your tools of the trade." Taking her hand, she led her to where they could get to the body without having to go near the reporters. Using Brian's shoulder to steady herself, she lifted one foot, slipped the bootie on, and stepped over the crime tape. Repeating the process with the other, she then helped Brian put her own booties on. Xe led the way with Brian walking directly behind her so as not to leave to many footprints or destroy vital evidence.

Approaching a lone officer, she asked him who all had been near the body. He told her that it had just been him, another officer and the chief.

"In that bag is a UV light, do you think we'll be able to pick anything up?"

Brian looked at the area surrounding the body, turning her head and using her senses to pick up humidity and the movement of air, she gave Xe a small grin. "We just might, the weathers perfect to preserve certain evidence. Let me check and see if he left us anything." She pulled the UV light out, started at the ankles, and worked her way up. She stopped and looked over her shoulder at Xe who was standing there with a notebook in her hand. "You gonna be my secretary?"

"Yep, just tell me what to do."

Brian wiggled her brows and gave her a lecherous grin. "Take your clothes off."

A dark brow rose to bury itself in her bangs. "Excuse me but how is that going to help with me taking notes?"

"Oh it's not to help you, it's to help me. I think better when I'm around gorgeous naked women." She snickered when the uniformed officer choked and walked away. "Works every time," She flashed Xe a grin. "OK, looks like we have some semen in the navel area. That's a first for this guy; he must have been in a hurry." Moving the light on the insides of the victim's thighs, she stopped when a small spot glowed bright purple. "We have some more on the inside to the upper left thigh, two millimeters from pubic bone. She searched the entire body and found just small spots of semen that had not been washed away. After scraping the samples into a small glass bottle, she gently turned the body over and with the use of a small flashlight and the spotlights angled toward her. She found a blonde pubic hair. Placing it into a plastic evidence bag, she handed it to Xe. With close examination to the amputated areas, she knew that it was the same guy from before that had dumped this body. She got up from where she has squatting and led Xe off to the side away from prying ears. Pulling her down to her, she whispered in her ear. "He's getting sloppy; he shaved her pubic hair like the others, nicked the Hell out of her and missed some spots. This body belongs to a brunette, so either the blonde pubic hair is his or it belongs to one of the other victims. I won't know until I can look at it under a microscope and do a DNA test."

"OK, let's bag this one and get her out of here, the autopsy can wait until later this morning." After giving the evidence to Boggs to be logged and then sent off to the labs. They helped the paramedics place the body into the ambulance and gave them instructions to what storage drawer to put it in. Shedding the booties and gloves, they placed them into a small bio bag and put everything back into the trunk. "Let's go home I'm exhausted and my hip is killing me." Xe handed the car keys to Brian and then limped to the passenger side and crawled in. Brian looked at the keys and grinned, she had always wanted to drive a cop car.

"Can I speed?"

"I'd prefer it, I wanna get home and collapse into bed," She saw Brian's face fall a bit. "With you." She finished and saw a glimmer of a smile cross Brian's face before she pulled the cruiser onto to RT. 340 and headed home.

****

After letting Bear out, filling both of her dishes and leaving their cell phones purposely on the kitchen table, they headed for the bedroom. Xe had shed all of her clothes before she had even gotten to the bed. Dropping face first into bed, she rolled onto her side and waited for Brian.

65

Fighting to keep her eyes open, she lost the battle the second a warm body snuggled up against her. Brian lay facing Xe; she traced a dark brow with her fingertip and leaned forward to kiss her parted lips. Snuggling closer to the detective's body, she laid her head on a muscular shoulder and drifted off to sleep. With the comfort of each other's arms wrapped around them and a warm furball nestled against the backs of Brian's thighs, they slept deeply for the first time in years. The ringing of the phone could not wake them; it rang for 20 minutes straight before stopping. Finally, the caller got fed up and decided to pay the women a visit. It didn't really bother Boggs that he would have to drive out to Xepher's house, he felt as if she were one of his daughters. He knew that when he had seen her the night before that she was exhausted from the long hours working the case. He also noticed that a tell tale sign of her exhaustion was that she would start to limp and favor her left leg. He would never forgive himself for not listening to her when she had told him of how her partner of two years was mentally unstable. He had just chalked up her partners problems as job stress and long hours. He had no idea that the man would kill his wife and mother in-law and then shot Xepher in the attempt to take his own life. He had asked her if she wanted a new partner when she had come back to work, the answer he got from her still made his hair stand on end. The low keening growl that she made had every one with in hearing distance cringing under their desks. He made it a point to never ask her that question again and took it upon himself to be her partner when she needed help. The other higher ups of the police station called him her little pet, but knew that she really didn't need a partner. They also knew that guilt was the reason Boggs was going out of his way and out onto a limb for her. So here, he was at ten o'clock in the morning pounding on her front door. If she didn't answer, he was tempted to crawl through the doggy door at the back of her house. The only problem with that idea was, he wasn't the thin man he used to be. It would be the embarrassment of a lifetime to be found wedged in the small door.

****

"Go way." Xe mumbled into the soft flesh beneath her cheek. "Damn pounding. Kill someone." Bringing a hand up to cover her ear, she felt fingers buried into her hair. Opening one eye half way, she took stock of where she was and recognized her bedroom. The odd thing was the pounding and a deep snoring. Picking her head up, she looked at the sleeping face of Brian. A smile came to her sleepy face as she looked into the calm innocent features of the woman that had worked her way into her heart. Then the smile vanished when a horrible snore rumbled in Brian's chest and a snorting noise came from her nose. Chuckling, Xe kissed her breast and tried to roll from her arms.

"No, can't leave." Brian mumbled and pulled Xe closer to her.

"Brian, someone's pounding on the front door."

"Kay." She let Xe go, got up from the bed and stumbled from the room. Xe lunged across the bed trying to catch her before she made it to the front door. Getting out of the bed, Xe's left leg gave out from under her and dropped her cussing to the floor. Boggs raised his hand and was about to pound on the door again when it cracked open to show a blurry green eye peeking back at him. Before he could say a word, the door was pulled open and a naked Brian walked away leaving the older man's mouth to drop open. Coming to his senses, Boggs stepped in and closed the door. Xe stumbled and limped from the bedroom, as she stepped into the living room, Brian walked up to her and wrapped her arms around her waist and pressed her face into her silk covered breasts. "Boggs." Was all she

67

said as she snuggled further into her body. A low groan came from Xe as she saw her boss coming further into the room; he raised his arms and shrugged his shoulders at her.

"She let me in, is she trying to give me a heart attack?" He watched as Xe struggled with her silk robe trying to wrap them both in it to cover Brian's bare ass. "I'll go make some coffee."

"Let me get Brian back to bed, I'll be there in a minute." She turned them around and half stumbled and walked them back to the bedroom. She couldn't believe that Brian had gone to the door completely naked, she looked down into her face and saw that she was sound asleep. "Ohh great, you're a sleep walker." A wicked grin came to her face along with an equally wicked thought. "Wonder what else you do while still asleep?"

"Would have found out if he hadn't shown up." She proved her point by taking a hardened nipple between her lips and nipping the end. Xe let out a low moan and sunk to the edge of the bed taking Brian with her.

"Ohh fuck." She threw her head back and moaned when a warm tongue circled her nipple. "He's a dead man!"

Brian released her nipple and placed a warm wet kiss between her breasts. "Go see what he wants; I'll be out in a minute." She pulled the silk robe around Xe. "I really hate you Xe." She gave her a kiss that had her gasping for breath and wishing Boggs wasn't in the kitchen. With all the strength she had left in her body, she left a very tempting Brian to get dressed. Taking a deep calming breath, she walked into the kitchen to find Boggs toasting bagels.

"Now I know why you didn't answer the phone or your door." He turned and handed her a cup of coffee. "I don't blame you one bit." He took a cup of coffee and sat down at the table, his eyes sparkling with laughter.

Xe sat down at the table and took a sip of the hot brew, her pale eyes still a little unfocused. "I didn't hear the phone, and we were just sleeping." She arched a brow at him. "Why am I explaining this to you? Anyway, we were exhausted. I think I've had eight hours total sleep in the last week."

"That's one of the reasons I'm here. I'm giving you the day off."

"Boggs, I have interviews to do, people to find and a shit load of reports to go over." Xe looked over her shoulder when she heard the shuffling feet of a still sleepy Brian come into the kitchen, taking in the clothes she was wearing sent a fire to her nether region. Brian was wearing only a button down shirt that Xe had left laying across the foot of the bed and a pair of her socks. Brian wrapped an arm around her neck and settled in her lap, burying her face against her neck, she mumbled something and fell back to sleep.

"That's one of the reasons you have the day off, the other one is you look like shit. I can't afford to have you getting sick." He leaned back in the chair and grinned at her pensive face. "You two are exhausted and trying to work that way can get you both hurt or worse." Leaning forward on one hand, he captured her eyes with his. "I pulled two detectives off their cases to comb the campsites, C&O canal and track down anyone who might have seen something. I put a rush on the lab reports and called Quantico for help with profiling. And I have an interview with the parents of the woman Brian identified. That leaves you two to sit here all day and come up with some ideas." He refilled his cup and filled one for a now wide awake Brian. "You might want to track down the next of kin for Dr. Blane. I think he has a sister nearby." She took a deep breath and shook her head in amazement, never had anyone done anything like this for her before.

"Why are you helping me?"

Boggs tried to hide the blush that was creeping up his face. "You remind me of my eldest daughter Sarah, you're headstrong like her. She always tells me that I don't pay attention to what goes on around me and I half listen to what I'm told. I wasn't listening like I should have when you came to me about your partner. I feel responsible for you getting shot."

"Damn it Dennis, I got myself shot." She reached across the table and took his hand. "I went in there with out calling for back-up, I knew what he had done and that he was dangerous. But being the stubborn ass that I am, I thought I could handle it. I was wrong. I thought I could talk him out of using the rifle on himself, I never expected him to shot me and then take his own life." She took a calming breath and leaned her head against Brian's. "He wanted to die no matter if he took every one with him in the process."

"Xe, you did what's in your nature to do." Brian cupped the side of her face in the palm of her hand. "You can't go against what your gut tells you. Your partner didn't want you dead, if that was the case he would have shot you in the chest or head."

"I know but it's still hard to accept that I couldn't stop it."

"Listen to Doc, your partner would have gone to prison for the rest of his life. All those guys you two put away would have gotten to him and that life would have been worse than killing himself. There was nothing you could do but if I had listened to you maybe I could have gotten him some help."

Brian held up her hands for them to stop. "Hold up you two, neither one of you is to blame, the man had some serious problems and neither one of you is to blame for that. So throw the guilt out the window and let us get this new psychopath off the streets, OK?" She looked between the two blushing people and smacked her hands together. "Let's go for breakfast, I'm starving."

****

Boggs was amazed at the amount of food that the two women could put away, he asked them why they just didn't pull their chairs up to the all you can eat bar and have at it. Brian grinned between him and Xe and spoke what was on her mind. "If we did that, I wouldn't have as much fun listening to Xe growl at me every time I stole food off her plate." She looked over to Xe's plate and stole the last bite of her blueberry muffin and got growled at. "See what I mean."

"You're a Hell of a lot braver than I am." He glanced between the two and could swear that he saw some kind of deep connection between them. "How long have you two known each other?" He asked seriously.

Xe looked to Brain who shrugged her shoulders. "Seems like a life time instead of about a week." Taking a piece of bacon off Brian's plate, she bit it in half and offered the remaining piece to her. She bit down on her bottom lip to keep from moaning when a wet tongue teased her fingertips. Boggs coughed and cleared his throat; he had never seen anything so seductive in his life. He had to get away from the two women before he made an ass of himself. Maybe lunch at home with his wife would be a nice change. Tossing some bills on the table, he pushed back his chair and stood.

"I've got some work to do, let me know if you two find out anything." He gave them both a wave and walked away towards the door thinking he would definitely go home for lunch, it was the sight of a small hand playing with the detective's zipper on her Levi's that got him. Xe rested her chin on her closed fist and locked eyes with a smirking medical examiner.

"Brian, what do you think of making love in public?"

"Don't know I've never done it in public, why?"

"Because if you don't stop playing with my zipper, I'm gonna throw you on top of the table and clear this place out with your screams."

Brian winked at her, then set a blazing fire down below by dragging her blunt fingernails up the seam of Xe's Levi's. "I'm game if you are." She teased her relentlessly until Xe couldn't take anymore and grabbed her hand.

"Come on we have work to do, we can play later and I'll warn you." She purred into Brian's ear. "I have great stamina and I play rough." Brian had to will her legs to hold her up; just the sound of that deep purring voice sent her senses racing wildly through her body.

****

They were sitting in Xe's small office at home going over the files of Dr. Blane. He had never really connected with anyone at the Hospital and very rarely spoke to the other doctor's, he was what every one thought of as the stereotypical ghoulish medical examiner. Xe cast a sideways glance at Brian and shook the thoughts from her head. "No I don't, never will and that is soo gross! I can't believe you think that of me!" She slugged Xe in her shoulder.

"What?" Xe whined and rubbed her stinging shoulder.

"Dead things, that's what."

Shivering, Xe rubbed her arms and gave Brian a strange look. "Did you just like read my mind or something?"

Brian raised just her eyes from what she was reading. "Believe me, it lasted a whole minute if that ,quite empty up there if you get rid of all the perverted stuff."

"Perverted stuff, I'm not the one who plays with dead stuff. Do you read tea leaves too?"

"No I prefer reading blood stains on maxi pads." She looked up when she heard a low groan and a thump, Xe was spread eagle on the floor from where she had fallen out of her chair. Her eyes closed tightly, she mumbled something unintelligible. Brian slowly slunk from her chair and crawled across the floor on her hands and knee's. Easing between Xe's spread legs, she crawled up the tall detective's body until she was hovering over her moving lips. She didn't know what it was about this woman but she brought out the worst in her. Ducking her head, she captured Xe's pink lips with her own; they still tried to move until she bit down on the full bottom lip and stroked it with the tip of her tongue. The second they stopped moving, she released her teeth and explored her lips with her tongue. Large hands came up to caress her ribs and graze the sides of her breasts. A deep moan rumbled between them when Brian lowered her body to lie completely on top of Xe. Deepening the kiss, Brian slowly teased Xe's tongue with her own, every shared breath brought them closer to what they both wanted and needed. When lights flashed before Brian's eyes from lack of air, she broke the kiss and buried her face against a warm neck that held the scent of Obsession and a hint of sandalwood soap. Xe's voice was deep and rough, her breathing ragged from the emotions Brian stirred in her with just a kiss. "Do you have any idea what you do to me?"

"I can imagine ya know what I want to do?"

"Take advantage of me and make me your love slave?" That quickly brought up Brian's head.

"You don't strike me as the submissive type."

"I'm not, I'm more of the...you ain't getting me till I'm ready." She rolled Brian off her and took off running through the house with Bear barking at her heels. Brian lay on the floor with her mouth hanging open; she couldn't believe what had just happened. Getting to her feet, she ran though the house and out the back door. Xe was nowhere in sight. Looking around, she heard the squeak of a door and then Bear whining from inside.

"What the Hell is she doing?" Going back in the

house, she stopped and listened for noises.

"You looking for me?" A deep purring came to her ear; strong arms wrapped around her from behind and pulled her into a warm body. She gasped when hands went under her shirt. Xe's large hands cupped her breasts and rough thumbs ran across her nipples bringing them to a hard peak. Moaning from the attention lavished on her nipples, she pushed her rear into Xe and rubbed against her. She felt Xe's body shudder against her and was then picked up and carried to their bedroom. What she saw excited her beyond anything she had ever experienced. Only candles lit the room and the soft fragrance of lavender hung in the air, a silky silver sheet covered the bed and sparkled in the candle light. Gently, Xe laid her down on the bed. A whisper of a touch trailing from her collar bones down to her bare feet. The look in Xe's dark and passion-filled eyes, glimmering with silver flecks in the candlelight made Brian's blood boil. She slowly undressed and dropped her clothes to the floor to let the candle light play across her bronzed flesh. Brian's breath lodged in her chest when large hands moved up to unfastened her Levi's and eased them down her body with just a brief touch of fingertips on her heated skin. Thumbs massaged her insoles and brought a low moan from her and sent shivers up her spine when they softly trailed to her ankles and massaged her calves. Her muscles jerked when a wet tongue joined fingertips and then lips, her fingers dug into the covers on the bed as Xe worked her way up each leg with her lips and teeth, nipping her skin lightly then kissing it. Each time she stopped dangerously close to her throbbing nether lips, she could feel her wetness soaking into the silk of her blue silk French cut panties. Xe, crawled up to straddle her hips and helped her to sit up, slowly pulling her t-shirt over her head, she placed kisses from the edge of her panties all the way up to the hollow of her throat. After the shirt hit the floor, she captured Brian's lips in the slowest most passionate kiss she had ever had. Xe's tongue filled her mouth and moved sensuously across her own, deep moans were exchanged as hands trailed across warm flesh. Memorizing textures shapes and causing tingles to travel through nerve endings. Brian felt like she was being worshiped, none of her other lovers had treated her like this, with the slow exploration of her entire body and gentle touches. After she was lowered back onto the bed, hands turned to satin as they drifted down her upper chest to cup the weight of her breasts in their palms. Arching her back to offer more of herself to her lover, she let out a long moan when a warm wet tongue traced her from neck to ear and circled the shell before slipping inside. A warm rush of juices flowed from between nether lips and soaked through her panties to coat her inner thighs. "What...are you...doing...to me?" She gasped out when teeth nipped at the sensitive flesh below her ear.

Her voice deep and sultry, Xe answered breathlessly into her ear. "Loving you." Brian buried her fingers in to thick dark hair and pulled her lips back to her, she kissed her deeply and with a hunger, she had never felt before. Xe pulled away, trailed open mouth kisses down the center of her chest, and stopped. Gazing into darkened green eyes, she ran a fingertip across kiss-bruised lips. "I love you Brian." She said softly before dropping her head down to circle a hardened nipple with the tip of her tongue. She felt fingers massage her scalp and then pull her back up to waiting lips. The hunger of before was gone and replaced with an intensity that came straight from the soul. Brian's hands ran down her shoulders to her back to stop at her hips. She kneaded the tight muscles of her ass, pulled her closer to grind her wet center into her slowly. Moaning deeply, Xe broke the kiss, and moved down to capture a nipple between her lips while rolling her other nipple between thumb and forefinger. She sucked until Brian thrust her hips upward.

"Please Xe!" She ground out from between clenched teeth. Switching to the other nipple, Xe sucked harder until her lovers back arched off the bed. The low moans had her wetter than she had ever been and so close to going over the edge that she had to squeeze her thighs together to control herself. Groaning deep in her chest, she licked the underside of a firm breast and down the side of Brian's ribcage. Brian was panting and pressing her center into her lover. Placing her hands on Xe's wide shoulders, she pleaded and pushed her lower. "I need you Xe...please touch me." She pleaded and let out a gasp when a wet tongue slipped beneath the waistband of her panties. Slowly, Xe slid the silk down her thighs until she could push them all the way off with her foot. She locked eyes with her lover and moved to lie between her thighs. Running her fingers across her lower stomach, she played with the short dark curls. Spreading her lips, she watched her lover's center pulsate with need.

"You're so wet baby." Blowing warm air across her center sent Brian to undulate her hips. The scent of her arousal made Xe's mouth water. Keeping eye contact, she reached out with her tongue and licked at a swollen nether lip. By drawing her tongue back and forth slowly, she was driving Brian insane. Xe stopped what she was doing and gazed with love-filled eyes in to misty green. "Tell me baby."

"Oohh Gods Xe...I love you...please!" Her hips jerked upward when Xe slipped her tongue between her lips and licked the juices from her. A deep moan vibrated her engorged clit; she could feel her muscles tense and start to roll from her chest downward. Xe slipped two fingers into her center, pulled her clit between her lips, and sucked. Slowly moving her fingers in and out, she tilted them upward, pressed into the sensitive area, and pushed Brian over into an earth-shattering release. With her name echoing off the walls, she plunged her tongue into a clutching center and drank what her lover offered and sent her back over the edge with another scream. Panting from holding back her own release, she crawled up Brian's twitching body and straddled her thigh. Capturing gasping lips, she kissed Brian with all the pent up arousal in her body and thrust her swollen womanhood against her thigh. Jerking her lips away, she threw her head back, her body arched and her release tore through her. Xe's cries of release took Brian with her. Bodies still trembling with aftershocks, they lay wrapped around each other. Xe raised her head when she heard sobbing. Wiping the tears from Brian's face with a fingertip, she kissed her cheeks of their moisture.

"Baby what's wrong?" She asked with a low whisper, pressing her face into Xe's neck she cried softly. "Baby did I hurt you?" Xe was beginning to worry that she had done something wrong. Tears filled her eyes and she cried silently. Brian lifted her tear stained face and saw the tears trailing down her cheeks.

"Ohh Gods no you didn't hurt me," You did something to me that no one ever has; you broke through my walls and captured my heart and soul." She cupped Xe's face with her hand and wiped the tears from her cheek with her thumb. "I love you Xepher Sallano. Even when I tell you that I hate you, I love you more than I can put into words." She kissed her softly and moaned when she tasted herself on her lover's lips. "I'll show you for the rest of our lives." She rolled over on top of her lover and showed her what was in her heart for the rest of the day and night until they fell exhausted into the land of dreams.

****

Xe moaned someone was licking the scar over her hip. Cracking one eye open, she saw the top of a tousled blonde head. Her hips jerked when Brian licked the area beside the strip of dark curls. "Ohh Gods I hope you're awake."

"Oohh I'm awake and very ready just like you are." She proved her point by dragging her fingers through Xe's wetness and then licking her fingers clean. Xe moaned and covered her eyes with her hands.

"Please wait just two seconds, I have to go…" She pointed towards the bathroom.

"Be quick or I'll start without you." She wiggled her brows when sleepy blue eyes looked at her. Xe fumbled with the sheet and hurried to the bathroom, she couldn't help but picture her lover touching herself. Her center twitched and her nipples hardened, after relieving herself, she rushed back to bed to see Brian with a lifelike thigh strap-on. What she was doing with it almost sent Xe to her knees, she was lying on her back, knees bent and her legs spread apart. Her wetness glistening on the insides of her thighs and the tip of the dildo, a deep guttural groan rushed from Xe's throat. She kneeled on the foot of the bed and licked her lips her voice dropped an octave. "Do it baby, push it in." Dark blue eyes watched as trim hips lifted and the dildo was slowly pushed into her lover's center. Xe's hips jerked forward, juices poured from her center as it clenched. She looked into dark green eyes before going back to watch the dildo slid in and out of her center. Her wetness coating its latex surface made Xe's mouth water.

"Xe touch yourself."

"Ohh Gods!" She moaned when her fingers slid through her own wetness, her hips pushed forward into her hand forcefully until she was steadily grinding to the same tempo of the dildo moving inside of her lover. She crawled the short distance to Brian with her fingers buried deep inside herself, she ground her hips as she leaned down and licked her lover's engorged clit. Brian tangled her fingers into thick dark hair and thrust her hips upward.

"So close…Come with me Xe!" She couldn't hold

back anymore, a low keening sound tore from her lips as she went over.

"Bri…ooohhh…Gods!" Xe thrust her hips once more and fell forward across her lover as her release ripped threw her. Gasping with each tremor, it was long minutes before she could catch her breath. Rolling onto her side, she placed a kiss on Brian's mound and sighed. "I swear baby you're gonna kill me." She slowly pulled the dildo from inside her and placed a gentle kiss to her pulsing center. "We won't be able to walk after what we've been doing."

"Plan on it." Brian growled. She moved out from under her lover and buried her face between her thighs, low moans came from her lips as she licked and sucked at her lover's juices.

****

Screams echoed threw the small house as they climaxed together. A low growling came from the kitchen and then sharp barking joined in. Bear was under the kitchen table barking at the man who was trying to fit through the doggy door. He had one arm and part of his shoulder through but couldn't get any further. Spittle flew from his lips as he struggled; he needed to end the sin coming from the other part of the house. The women's screams of pleasure tore at his brain; it was un-natural what they were doing. Their blood needed to be spilt so that they could be free of sin, he had followed them and waited until it was time to take the blonde away and make her a sacrifice to his God. Now he would have to wait, he used his other arm and pushed himself backward with all the strength he had. A scream bubbled on his lips as the metal of the doggy door tore into the tender under part of his upper arm. The sound of ripping material and the clatter of the doggy door was all Xe heard as she ran into the kitchen. "Bear? Bear where are you?" She called and looked under the table to see her small dog cringing with the hair going down the center of her back standing on end. Her legs still shaky from her climax, she sunk to her knees in weakness. "What was it girl?" She asked trying to catch her breath. Looking to where the doggy door was still swinging, she saw a piece of dark blue material and drops of blood on the floor. "BRIAN!" She yelled in panic when she heard glass shattering from the other room. Getting to her feet, she ran to where the noise had come from. She stopped in the living room to see Brian standing near the windows that ran along the side of the front door. In Brian's hands was a baseball bat that she kept behind the door, glass lay across the floor in jagged pieces around her feet. "Don't move baby." Grabbing her boots from near the couch, she slipped her feet into them and walked around as much of the glass as she could. Swinging Brian up into her arms, she carried her to the couch. "What happened?" She asked while cupping her silent lover's face.

"Some bastard punched his hand through the window." Tear filled eyes connected with blue. "I smacked his arm with this." She held the bat up. "Xe?" She whimpered and fell into her arms. "It was him wasn't it?"

"I think so," She hugged her lover tightly to her chest. "I have to call Boggs."

****

The house was full of evidence techs, uniformed officers and Boggs. He had cruisers patrolling the area looking for the man who had tried to get in to Xe and Brian's house. Who ever this man was, he was escalating in his killings and Boggs was afraid that he had now set his sights on either Sallano or Dr. Meadows. His MO had changed as well, none of the other victims had been taken from houses, if they had, he was sure that someone would have placed a missing persons report instead of them having two unidentified bodies at the morgue. He had to literally throw Sallano out the front door of her house along with Meadows and her furball dog. He didn't want them at the house incase the nut case came back, he would have two officers staying inside her house while the rest of them tried to find the nut. Giving Sallano the address of Dr. Blane's next of kin, he told her to go question the woman and see if he had spoken to her about the serial of murders.

****

Brian started humming the theme song from *Psycho;* she looked up at the huge house waiting for *Norman Bates* to pop up in a window somewhere. Shivers ran down her spine from the sight of the dilapidated two-story house. The grass was knee high, paint faded and peeling from warped wooden siding, singles blown off and looking like small horns on the roof and the front porch sagging from rotten wood. "Xe are you sure this is the place? I mean, who in the Sam hell would live here?"

"Yep, it's the place." She looked down at the paper from Boggs. "Says here that there are bodies stacked like firewood in the guest bedroom."

"Oohh YeeeHaaa, let's have a BBQ!" Brian rolled her eyes at her lover. "Can we just burn down the eyesore and forget about going in there?"

Xe turned in her seat and gave Brian the raised eyebrow look. "Are you afraid to go in there?"

Brian crossed her arms over her chest, glared and Xe and replied in a strong voice. "Yes God damn it, I'll have you know that I missed the ending of *Silence of the lambs* because it was so damn spooky!" She raised her left eyebrow at her lover. "I may have drooled over *Jodi Foster,* but when it came to all those bugs and the pitch black basement!" She shivered and rubbed her arms.

"I'll protect you baby," Moving across the seat, she gave her lover a deep intense kiss that left her eyes closed and her breathing ragged. "Let's get in there and talk to who ever falls out of the shadows."

"Nothing like embedding thoughts of horror." Brian mumbled. Xe opened the passenger side door and helped her lover out, taking her hand; they walked up to the front door skirting the rotten boards and holes. Xe took a deep breath, knocked on the wooden door, and waited. "If Norman answers, run like hell."

"Gee thanks for the oohh mighty warrior façade you gave me earlier, big damn chicken."

Xe leaned in close and licked her ear. "But I'm your big chicken." She quickly pulled away with embarrassment when the door opened and a nurse stepped onto the porch. "I'm Detective Sallano and this is Chief Medical Examiner Meadows, is Mrs. Gaston home?"

"Yes, she's in but I'm not sure she'll be able to help you." She said in a low voice.

"Why is that?" Brian stepped in front of her lover. "This is rather important."

"Well, you can try but she's been unresponsive verbally for over a year now. She suffered several strokes that left her paralyzed and in a wheelchair." She showed them into the large house and then to the small room where Mrs. Gaston was staring off into space. Brian latched onto Xe's hand in a death grip, she hated houses like this one and was not about to leave her lover's side for nothing.

"Can I speak to you for a minute?" Xe asked the nurse, then pried her hand free from Brian's, and asked her to check on Mrs. Gaston's health.

Brian growled at her. "Don't you leave me!"

"Never baby, I'll be right here." She pulled the nurse to the side but kept Brian in her peripheral vision. "I'm investigating the murder of Mrs. Gaston's brother Dr. Blane; did he ever come here to visit her, call or anything?"

"He would come by once a week and check on her. He never stayed long; he and his nephew didn't get along. They disagreed on Mrs. Gaston's care."

"She has a son? Where can I find him?" Xe's mind grabbed onto the bit of information.

"He doesn't get home from work until five o'clock, and then he takes over her care." She lowered her voice so that Mrs. Gaston wouldn't hear her. "That guy gives me the creeps, looks at me with weird eyes."

"Really?" A dark brow rose. "What's this guy's name?"

"Jeffrey Gaston, he owns that Jeff's lawn care service that does all the banks and big businesses in Frederick."

"What kind of car does he drive and what does he look like?"

"A big dark blue thing, not sure what it is but it's huge and has one of those big antennae's on it." She thought for a few seconds then continued. "I'd say he's a little shorter than you, maybe weighs around 175lb, bald, eye color is hard because his eyes are all squinty, I'd take a guess and say hazel. And he wears those clothes like farmers do you know green work clothes. You would think that he would at least cut that jungle of a yard out there, the funny thing is I've never seen him dirty after cutting grass all day. You know grass stained boots or clippings on his pant legs."

"You would think huh?" Xe replied and knew from cutting her own grass that she ended up looking like Kermit the frog after a short time.

****

Brian kneeled across from Mrs. Gaston and waved her hands in front of unmoving eyes. Snapping her fingers near her ears received the same response, none. Looking on the small table beside the chair, she noticed numerous bottles of medicine. Picking a couple up, she read the labels, opened the bottles to look at the pills and moaned. The pills in the bottles did not match what the label read. She wondered why the woman was taking those types of meds. "Haladol, Prozac and Demerol, something's not right here." She pushed up the older woman's sleeve and let out a low groan. "Xe...Detective Sallano can I see you a minute?" She watched her lover limp towards her, her heart sped up a beat at the sight of the beautiful woman that was all hers. Then remembered what she was doing and sighed. "Look at her wrists, this woman does not need to be tied down. She has a catheter and a colostomy bag and is pumped full of enough drugs to keep the local nut ward sleeping for a week!" She looked to the nurse standing beside her lover. "What meds do you give her while you're here?"

"I just make sure that her bags are empty and that she's comfortable. I was never instructed to administer any meds."

"What about in case of an emergency, who's her doctor on record?" Brian was reeling with the information she knew to be a little iffy

"I'm supposed to call Mr. Gaston at work and tell him. He never told me anything about who her doctor is." She took a deep breath. "Listen, I know this all looks bad me being a nurse and everything. I work for a nursing service, we do in home care and that is it. Anything else is done by the person who hires us."

Brian waved a hand at her and smiled. "It's OK, I know how this all works, I'm not blaming you."
Xe's facial expressions became pensive; she walked over to the medicine bottles and started looking at the labels. She was no doctor but some of them looked a little suspicious to her. Looking back to the nurse, she saw that she was occupied with Brian. Palming one of the bottles closet to

Mrs. Gaston, she rejoined her lover. She rested a hand on her shoulder. "Brian, you ready to go?"

"Yeah Xe I am, I have some paperwork to do at the office." She held out a hand to the nurse. "Thank you for all your help."

* * * * * * * * * * * *

Xe drove like a bat out of hell towards the hospital, a mischievous look was firmly planted on her face.

"Alright Xe, what are you up to?"

"What makes you think that I'm up to something?" She glanced quickly to her lover and grinned.

"That look says so, what did you do?"

She reached into her pocket and pulled out the bottle of pills. "I wanna run it for finger prints, from what Nurse Ratchet described, Jeffrey is a strange bird and he may need his wings clipped."

"Isn't what you did like sorta illegal?"

"Only if I get caught, besides what you did last night is illegal in some states."

Brian's eyes grew huge; her mouth fell open to make a small coughing noise. "Me! What about you?"

"I didn't cuff you to the headboard."

"That's 'cuz you didn't think of it," She stuck her tongue out at her. "I'll do worse later."

* * * * * * * * * *

Brian scanned all the admittance records for the last year and none of them was for Mrs. Gaston. She then did the same for Jeffrey Gaston and found an ER admittance for seven months prior for a tetanus shot. "Patient cut palm of left hand on wire, six sutures to close, prescribed an antibiotic cream by Dr. V. Lundel MD." Getting up from her desk, she went into the small room where Xe was going

85

over case files that Boggs had given her. Slowly opening the door, she found her lover lying on the small bed, folder open on her chest and sound asleep. Pushing off her worn out tennis shoes, she pulled her t-shirt over her head and dropped it to the floor and then her Levis. Taking the folder from Xe's chest, she placed it on the small table and crawled into the bed beside her. Snuggling up to her side, she laid her head on her shoulder and fell asleep.

****

Two hours later, Xe woke with a start. She had the strangest feeling that someone had been looking at her while she slept. Looking around the room, she saw that the door to the room was open. She leaned up on an elbow and then looked down to see that Brian was still asleep. Easing out from under her half-naked lover, she kissed her gently on her parted lips and then got out of the bed. Slowly walking towards the door, she eased it open further and looked down both ends of the hallway. Closing her eyes, she concentrated on hearing anything out of the ordinary. Walking across the hall to Brian's office, she looked in to see the place trashed. Every file folder was on the floor, the PC's tower was pried open with wires cut and what was left of Brian's lab coat lay across the desk with a letter opener sticking out of where it had been jabbed into the desktop. Running back to the small room, she woke her lover. "Brian get up, he's been here!" She shook her shoulder until green eyes shot open.
"Who's been here?" She asked groggily.
"The psycho, he tore your office apart, come on we have to get out of here and to my office." Xe was collecting her files when she heard Brian using sentences with words that didn't quite belong together. Looking over her shoulder, she saw that her lover was holding up a t-shirt and one shoe. "Baby what's wrong?"

86

"That fuckinggoodfornothingsonofabitchinasshole-
cocksucker stole my CLOTHES!"

It took Xe a few seconds to figure out what came
before the 'stole my clothes' part. Getting to her feet, she
pulled her lover into her arms and held her tight. "I'm just
glad that you were in here with me when he showed up,"
She tilted her face up to her. "I don't know what I would
have done if anything happened to you."

"Right now I'm more dangerous than he could ever
dream of being!" After pulling, a pair of scrubs on, she and
Xe went out the back door of the morgue. 25 minutes later,
they were pulling into the police station parking lot. This
would be the first time that Brian had been to Xe's office,
for some reason that drilled into her mind that she was in
fact in a lot of danger. Before it was a subconscious thought
but now, that had all changed when she walked in to the
building filled with police officers. Taking her lover's hand,
she stayed close to her side as they wove their way to Xe's
office. They stopped on their way to see Boggs and then
went to the area where they took fingerprints. Pulling the
pill bottle from her pocket, she handed it to the officer at
the small table. "I need prints on this now! When you have
them, run them through the computer. I think that's the
psycho stealing heads." The young officer looked into
steely eyes and nodded. "We need to check some things out
then we're going back to Mrs. Gaston's house." Brian
shuddered; she hated the idea of going back to the creepy
place. Tightening her grip on Xe's hand, she looked up into
eyes full of fury and nodded her head. They went to Xe's
small cubicle and pulled up any information that they could
find on the Gaston family. The only thing that they found
was that Mr. Eugene Gaston had died in 1977 due to
natural causes and that his survivors were his wife and son.
"Is having your head cut off considered natural causes?" Xe
asked sarcastically. "Gardening accident?" She pointed to

the screen where it told of how he had been found near a lawn mower with his head a few feet away. "What did he do stick his head under it and start the damn thing?" Brian stood behind her with one hand on her shoulder and her chin resting on the other.

"More like someone helped him loose his head."

"Talking about loosing heads little lady," A young detective junior grade stepped up to Brian. "How about loosing Sallano's and joining me for lunch." He leaned against the edge of Xe's desk and gave Brian a charming smile. Brian returned his smile, brushing her fingers against Xe's hand in a comforting manner; she turned to face the young man.

"I see only one problem with that," She dropped her voice to a sultry purr. "You see, Xepher here has the sexiest little head that I've ever seen. I love to take it between my teeth and feel it throb beneath my tongue when I bite down on it and then I run my tongue across it and flick the very end until she moans and thrusts against my lips. I suck on it until she wraps her beautiful thighs around my head." She let out a deep moan and watched his eyes grow darker. "Just the feel of it becoming engorged in my mouth makes me cum." She felt Xe shudder against her side; she let out a deep chuckle and looked down at the detective's crotch. "From the looks of the stain on your pants, I'd say you have a problem with premature ejaculation." The young detective stumbled away with his Jacket pulled in front of him. Brian was chuckling softly and leaning against her silent lover.

"That was cruel Brian," She ran her hand up the inside of Brian's thigh and felt her jump a little. In a very low whisper meant only for Brian's ears, she said. "He's not the only one that has a problem being premature."

"I'll make it up to you when we get home." She leaned against her lover's side and ran her fingers up her ribcage to stop right below her breast. "For hours." She whispered in her ear.

"Let's get out of here." She stood slowly, and pulled her pant legs down with a grimace, she gave Brian a low growl when she heard her snort. "S'not funny." She whined.

****

Boggs told them that he had back up set up if they needed it even though he didn't agree that Jeff Gaston was guilty of anything but being weird. The fingerprints on the man came back negative on any priors or warrants so he thought they were just jumping to conclusions. Not even Brian telling him her suspicions about the mother being over prescribed psychological drugs and the problem with Dr. Blane's lab results. On the other hand, the fact that she had been singled out by some whack job who stole her clothes earlier that day while she was sleeping, did have him raising his eyebrows. Xe wrapped an arm around her waist and pulled her close to her side as they walked out of the station house. "Don't worry about it baby, if it isn't him we'll keep looking. Let's stop at home so you can change and I can check on Bear."

****

After strapping on a bullet proof vest and pulling her t-shirt on, Xe pulled two Glock .9mm' from the safe in her office, checking the clips, she put them into her double holster and added extra clips to the leather pouches. Going to the bottom desk drawer, she pulled out a boot knife and strapped it to her calf under her pant leg. She hoped that she didn't need all of the stuff she was carrying but it was always better to be prepared than not at all. Leaving the office, she went to see if Brian was ready. She wasn't prepared for what she saw, her lover wore a bulletproof vest and had a holster at the small of her back along with her gold badge clipped to the front of her belt. To finish off her look, she pulled a black windbreaker on with Medical Examiner on the back in yellow letters.

"Baby since when do Medical Examiners carry guns?"

Green eyes lifted to hold pale blue, a small grin lifted the corner of her lips. "Ya know how the stiffs sit up on the tables? Well, a .38 is how I put them back down on the table. I'm a pretty good shot too: I only hit the oxygen tanks once so far."

Xe's eyes rolled upward, she knew she was in a shit load of trouble now. "Come on Dirty Harriet; let's go scare an old lady."

****

Jeff Gaston pulled his car around to the back of the house; he knew that he had taken a big chance on being at the morgue earlier that day but he had no choice. He had to make sure that the Medical Examiner didn't have anything on the missing women or his Uncle. Knowing that she had probably ordered new tests on him after his murder, he didn't want her to know that prior to his heart attack, he had been given Bella Donna in his coffee. Pulling the door to the cellar open, he then opened the trunk of his car and lifted the black body bag from the trunk. Carrying it down the steps, he dropped it into a corner and returned to his car three more times. When he was finished, he went into the house to check on his mother. Walking through the house, he stopped long enough to take the sling from his arm off and lay it on the cluttered kitchen table. As soon as his arm dropped to his side, a sharp pain tore through it. "Fucking little bitch!" He swore. "I'll fuck you with a baseball bat for breaking my arm." Placing a funny smile on his face, he went into the small room to dismiss the nurse for the rest of

90

the day. He couldn't understand the look on her face until he realized that he was dressed in a police officer's uniform instead of his usual green uniform. He saw recognition in her eyes, quickly he reached out and punched her in the face twice and watched her slump to the floor. Taking her by a foot, he dragged her towards the kitchen and left her lying in the middle of the floor until he could change out of the uniform.

* * * * * * * * * * * *

"Baby I really hate this house, I still say we should just have it burned to the ground and be done with it." Brian shivered as she looked up at the upper windows, she squinted her eyes when she saw movement in one of them. "I think Jeff's home early." She pulled Xe down and pointed to the upper window. "I saw him in that room."

"Let's go have a little talk with him." They walked slowly up to the door and skirted the new holes that were in the porch. Knocking on the door, they waited for someone to answer. A good ten minutes went by with no one answering. Xe shrugged her shoulders and motioned for Brian to follow her. They rounded the back of the house and saw the dark blue Crown Victoria sitting with the trunk open. Drawing her pistol, she motioned for Brian to stay behind her. Stepping next to the car, she looked inside and saw that it was empty. Moving to the trunk, she spun away and took a deep breath of air. Brian seeing her lover's face turn an unhealthy green became concerned.

"Xe what's wrong?"

"Take a good whiff and tell me what you think it is."

Brian stepped next to her and didn't even have to get close to know what the stench was. It was the combination of decomposing bodies, feces and formaldehyde.

"I think we have or guy Xe." She pulled her .38 from its holster and checked to make sure that a bullet was chambered before replacing it.

"Let me call for back up before we go in there." She pulled her cell phone from her belt and had her finger over the button to hit speed dial when a scream pierced the air and a sharp pain shot up her arm. Falling to the ground holding her shattered arm she watched her lover pull her .38 and fire at a retreating figure that had disappeared into the cellar doors. "Baby don't go down there!" She screamed as her lover charged down into the darkness. "Gods don't go down there..." She whimpered as the darkness claimed her.

****

Brian hugged the cellar wall as she slowly made her way down the wooden steps. Her vision still had not adjusted to the darkness; she stopped and waited a few moments until she could see a few glints of obstacles off to her left. Slowly taking a calming breath, she eased down the last step and into the pitch-black darkness. Running her hand against the wall, she tried to listen for any sound or feel any movement around her. A breeze blew past her face making her throw her head back; a loud thump hit the wall in front of her face. Dropping to her knees, she swung a foot out and felt her shin connect with something and then a low grunt came to her ears. Crawling on her hands and knees, she fell over something covered in plastic. Sliding on her stomach over what ever it was, she scurried away from it to hit her head against something made of metal. Warmness trailed down from her eyebrow and clouded what little vision she had. Wiping it away, she picked up the coppery scent of her blood. Reaching her hand up, she felt the cool metal of what she determined to be a table. Running her hand across it, she felt a jabbing pain in the tips of her fingers. Holding back a yelp, she clamped her hand over her mouth and stayed still. She knew that she would have to find a light switch or leave the cellar; her lover was outside injured and she was becoming worried when she hadn't joined her. Standing up, she raised her hand over her head to search for a pull cord. She thought she had found one until she felt the rubber on an extension cord. Stepping forward a few steps, she stopped when her toe hit a wall. She was about to search for a switch when a biting pain slashed across her upper thigh. Spinning she fell into the wall and fired into the dark. The echoing of her shoots made her drop her head and cringe; it saved her as she heard the impact of a weapon bounce of the wall near her head and a grunt of frustration. Aiming her .38, she fired again and heard a squeal of pain. Fumbling along the wall, she found a switch and flipped it on. The brightness blinded her; covering her eyes with her arm, she waited until she could remove it with out the sharp pain. Looking around the bright cellar, she saw a blood trail across the floor and to a set of steps across the vast space. Limping from the pain in her thigh, she went to the stairs and looked up at the open door. Slowly she took the steps and clenched her jaw to keep from screaming out.

****

Xe moaned and rolled to her back, the pain in her forearm was worse than when she had been shot. Rolling to her knees, she fell forward on to her good hand and lost what little bit of substance was in her stomach. Dry heaves racked her body, sweat poured down her face and into her burning eyes. She had to get up and look for her lover, she had a feeling that Brian was in serious danger. With her arm hanging useless at her side, she stumbled down the steps and looked around the large cellar. The sight of black body bags in a pile and the stench of the cellar made her stomach roll again.

****

Brian kneeled by the nurse's side and felt for a pulse in her neck, checking the dark purple bruise on her jaw and cheekbone, she knew that the woman was only unconscious and would be all right. Using the kitchen table to get to her feet, she slowly made her way through the gloomy house. She looked down at the floor and tried to follow the blood trail, noticing that it went towards where she had spoken to the nurse days before she stopped and listened for noises. The low drone of the TV and then a falsetto voice was heard coming from the small room.

"You finally did it this time Jeffrey! You are a filthy sinner and you must pay for your sins!" Brian shook with the sounds of a loud slapping sound and then whimpers. She sunk down the wall and listened to the one-way conversation. "NO erections! It's the devils way of controlling man!" Was screamed in a high voice and then a loud male voice screamed 'NO!'

Brian moved around the corner of the room and aimed her .38 at Jeffrey Gaston or whom she thought was the man. What looked to be a Halloween mask covered the face of the naked person before her. A shoulder length wig fell across wide shoulders and neck, breasts heaved as the person took gulping breaths as a hand clenched on the handle of a tree-trimming saw.

"Jeffrey put the saw down!" Brian said in a calming voice. "Just put it down and step back from your mother." She felt the hair rise on her neck and knew that her lover had just stepped behind her. "Xe he has a saw in his hand."

Ignoring the psycho, she was more concerned about her lover. "Are you OK baby?" She placed a large hand on her shoulder.

"Been better." She replied without taking her eyes away from the crazed person. "Do your cop thing and arrest

94

him or something." Before either of them could do anything, a loud scream of "Spill the sinner's blood!" echoed through out the room and then a loud scream of pain came from the crazed person. They watched as the saw moved at a downward angle and blood sprayed across the room and continued to fountain as the jerking body fell backwards. "Shit!" Xe yelled as she quickly moved past Brian and into the room. Covering her eyes, she shook her head and retreated from where the body was lying. "Can't help him baby." She wrapped her good arm around her lover's shoulder and led her through the house to where the nurse was just coming to. "He cut off his dick." She looked down into her lover's pale face and caught her before she fell to the floor. "Fuck baby you're hurt." She eased her down onto the floor, took off her belt and applied it above the slashed area of her thigh. Ripping her t-shirt off, she wrapped it around Brian's leg and told her not to move. Slapping the nurse lightly on her hands, she pulled her the rest of the way to be conscious. "I need your help, Brian's hurt."

****

Boggs face was white as alabaster, in all the years he was a cop he had never seen a more gruesome sight. When Xe had called and told him to send out the homicide team to the Gaston residence, he had no idea what they would be doing. As soon as he opened the door to Jeffrey's room, his stomach rebelled and he covered his shoes with his lunch. The stench of rotting flesh was as thick as fog. On the shelves across one entire wall were decomposing heads of half a dozen women. Brian and Xe turned their heads at the sight until they were able to control their own stomachs and enter the room. The heads sat upon the women's feet with their hands cupping their sunken cheeks. Sitting on a table next to a filthy blood covered bed was the head of Dr. Blane along with jars with human organs in them. Both women had seen enough and left the room to go outside for fresh air. Standing outside reading a leather bound journal, Xe skimmed over the pages until she came to a section where Gaston tells of the reason why he killed it uncle. He simply stated that his uncle had caught him in the morgue one night trying to steal a body, and when he threatened his life, Dr. Blane laughed at him. He knew that his uncle hated him for drugging his mother with his pills and for all the bodies he was defiling because he was as his uncle called him "A sick fuck" So to protect himself he had to get rid of the medical examiner. Closing the journal, she gave out a whistle through her teeth and handed it to Brian. Wrapping her uninjured arm around her shoulders, she placed a soft kiss to her lips. "Love you baby." She whispered to her as she rested her head against her shoulder.

"Love you to, let's get out of here." They watched as an ambulance left the driveway with the nurse and Mrs. Gaston inside. Now that they were free to leave, Xe helped her lover to the car and drove them to the hospital to be treated for their wounds. Xe wasn't worried about her arm as much as she was about Brian's leg. The weapon that had injured her was the saw that Gaston had used to severe body parts with. Brian told her not to worry that with the amount of blood she had lost that the wounds were clean. When the first ambulance had shown up, she had one of the paramedics give her a surgical scrub and used it to clean the wound to be on the safe side and to put Xe at ease.

****

"So baby, what are we gonna do on our forced vacation?" Xe asked as she plopped down on the couch.
"Ohh I don't know how about if we stay home lounge around the house naked and watch dirty movies on TV?" A dark eyebrow cocked above an amused eye, she

gave out a snort and fell back on the couch with a groan.

"We're already naked. Watch dirty movies, why would we do that?"

Brian lay down beside her and tapped the cast that went from her lover's upper arm to the tips of her fingers. "Ohh because my handicapped warrior, you're useless in plaster. And I want to watch dirty movies."

"Hey I'm not completely useless, my arms in a cast not my tongue! Dirty movies are dumb, I like the real thing." She wiggled her tongue and gave Brian the come-hither movement. "You still owe me from the other day."

A wicked grin split Brian's face; she crawled up Xe's body until she was kneeling over her face. "And I'll pay you back with interest." Her head fell back when she felt warm fingers run up the inside of her thigh and tangle in her short blonde curls. "Double interest!" She cried out when she felt her lover's tongue slip between her nether lips.

****

Boggs walked up to Xe and Brian's door with a huge grin on his face and a small black box in his hand. His wife had told him to wait and see them in a few days, give them some time alone and to heal. But he couldn't wait, he had to see Xe as soon as possible. Raising his fist to pound on the door, he stopped when he heard a blood-curdling scream through the open windows. Stepping back, he threw his shoulder against the front door and fell inward when the door jam gave way. Coming up onto one knee, he pulled his pistol and trained it around the living room. He let out a long gasp and covered his eyes. "Ohh Christ!" He mumbled.

"Damn it to Hell Boggs!" Xe rolled over on top of Brian to shield her lover's naked body. "What the Hell is wrong with you, and why'd you break our door down?"

97

Pulling the blanket off the back of the couch, she covered Brian up and got to her feet to smack Boggs on his head.

"OOWW! Why'd you hit me?" He looked up at her naked body, turned a bright red and dropped his eyes to the floor. "I heard god-awful screams and thought..." He stopped when he heard Brian laughing hysterically. "Oohh for the love of God, here this is yours I'm going home to hang my self from the rafters." After Boggs had left, Xe sat down on the couch and flipped the box over in her hand. Brian pulled her down to rest against her chest and took the box from her fingers. "What is it?"

"Don't know open it for me." A gasp came from Brian's lips after she opened the small box, she snapped it shut and placed it on her lover's chest. "What was it?" Xe asked.

"Ohh just a gold shield that has the word lieutenant across the top of it." She rolled out from under Xe and looked her in the eye. "Since that means a raise in pay, you can buy me a ring."

Xe blinked her eyes a few times. "A ring, what kind of ring do you want?"

Brian waved her right hand in front of her lover's face. "What kind of ring do you think I want?"

She dropped her dark brows over her nose and thought for a second. "Ohhh that kind of ring," She pulled Brian close and kissed her with all the emotion she had in her body and soul. "I love you Dr. Meadows, marry me."

"Under one condition...I get Bear." She snorted at the shocked look on her lover's face. "Just kidding," She placed a soft kiss on her lips. "I love you Xepher and yes I'll marry you. Now let's go to bed."

****

The uniformed officer drove past the address that the dispatcher gave him over the radio, so far that night they had received numerous calls about screams coming from one of the houses. A huge grin covered his face when he saw the Crown Victoria sitting in the driveway with a sign saying 'Just Joined' across the trunk. He knew who's car it was and there was no way in Hell that he was going to tell Sallano about the disturbing the peace tickets she was going to get, that was Boggs job. Before he pulled away, he heard a war cry that set the hair on his arms on end. Shivering he rolled up his windows, turned off his radio and sped off into the night.

The end

Order These Great Books Directly From Limitless, Dare 2 Dream Publishing

Humanz by Richard Ellis	17.00	SciFi-NEW
Pirate Justice:Kara's Story by j. taylor Anderson	17.00	Adventure-NEW
Poetry from the Featherbed by pinfeather	17.00	Poetry
A Woman's Ring by Rea Frey	16.00	NEW
Sweet Melody by Liana M. Scott	16.00	NEW
Still Life by Tracy Haisley	17.00	NEW
Walnut Hearts by Jackie Glover	17.00	NEW
Soldiers Now by Dean Krystek	16.00	November 2004
Sins of the Innocent by Deborah E. Warr	18.00	Mystery-NEW
Guardians of the Stone by Josiah Lebowitz	17.00	SciFi/Adventure NEW
Where Love is Not by Deborah E. Warr	16.00	Ellen Richardson Mystery-NEW
		Total

South Carolina residents add 5% sales tax.
Domestic shipping is $3.50 per book

Visit our website at: http://limitlessd2d.net

Please mail orders with credit card info, check or money order to:

Limitless, Dare 2 Dream Publishing
100 Pin Oak Ct.
Lexington, SC 29073-7911

Please make checks or money orders payable to **Limitless**..

Printed in the United States
25100LVS00006B/34

9 780976 076926